To JONATH

ENJOY YOUR TRIP TO...

A SCI-FI HORROR NOVEL

FRENZY ISLAND

You Rock!

RICHARD E. ROCK

CRANTHORPE
MILNER

STAY METAL

Rich E. Rock

First published by Cranthorpe Millner Publishers (2022)

ISBN 978-1-80378-069-6 (Paperback)

www.cranthorpemillner.com

Cranthorpe Millner Publishers

For Christine and Zeb

Chapter 1

Cynthia liked to get to Scottsdale Airport early to grab a hot dog and a coffee before flying out to the spaceport to start her shift. At this point in time it was a spaceport in name only, as nothing had officially been launched from there. The company were promising that commercial passenger flights skimming the Earth's atmosphere would be starting the next year. But then, they'd been repeating that promise for the last five. All that aside, no matter how far ahead of flight-time she arrived, there was always someone there before her, which only succeeded in pissing her off as it meant a queue at Gene's Hot Dog Heaven trailer.

"Usual, Cynth?" asked the man himself from behind the counter.

"Hell yeah!" Cynthia replied with a wicked grin. "S'always the right time for a dog."

"Thanks to people who hold that attitude, I can pay my rent," Gene said in his glorious Arizona drawl. He started preparing her usual jumbo cheese dog with onions, ketchup and mustard.

"Besides, when you work shifts like I do," Cynthia continued as she fished her wallet from her shoulder bag, "you stop caring if it's morning or night. Hunger is hunger, you know."

"Yeah, I guess. Have to take yer word for that though. Always bin a nine-to-five man, mysel'. Till now, o'course."

"You're living the dream there, Gene. Living the dream."

"Well, I don' know 'bout that."

Gene looked at his watch. It was pushing 7:20p.m. Be time to pack up and head home soon. When he'd left the house that lunchtime to come to work he'd made sure to leave a beer or two in the fridge for when he got back.

Cynthia zipped up her leather jacket. The sun had already disappeared behind the hills, leaving a dying blue sky behind it. She inhaled as the sweet aromas of coffee and frying onions mixed with the chilly breeze coming in from the desert.

By now a few more workers had shown up and were milling around. Cynthia spotted her friend and colleague Matt and nodded him a hello as a queue formed behind her. Not caring, she carried on yakking.

"Screw it. Gimme a donut too."

"That's my girl," Gene said with a wink. "Say, you'll never guess who came by here yesterday. Alice Cooper."

Cynthia was genuinely astounded. "What? No shit!"

"Yep. Sold 'im a dog before his flight. Had his wife 'n daughter with him. Nice fam'ly."

"Gene, you just officially became the coolest guy I know."

"'Bout time you cottoned on."

"What is it about Arizona that pulls the rock stars in?" Cynthia pondered aloud. "Place is crawling with 'em. We got Alice Cooper, Rob Halford from Judas Priest, the bassist from Megadeth, that dude from Tool."

"Two words," replied wise old Gene, "skies 'n golf. We got the best o'both."

A small passenger plane swished through the bleached-out sky overhead.

"Ooh! Looks like my ride is here," Cynthia said.

Gene handed over her coffee, hot dog and donut. Cynthia paid up, bade Gene a good evening and scurried off to the landing strip. She liked Gene. He never seemed to be afflicted by bad moods no matter what shit was going down. She admired this increasingly rare quality in a human being. Gene, in turn, watched as his favourite customer, laden with her dinner of saturated fats, salts, sugars and caffeine, trotted off for another long night of doing whatever the hell it was she did in that darn spaceport place.

Nice kid, he thought, *but if my daughter-in-law starts dressing like that, me an' her'll be having words.*

The aircraft, sleek, silver and not seen anywhere outside of the SpaceWurd corporation, taxied to a halt on the runway. The pilot opened the fuselage door and lowered the steps where a disorderly queue had formed.

"Good evening, minions," he grinned. "All set for another night of scrubbing floors and cleaning toilets?"

"Hey, Tyle, your flies 'r undone," piped up a wit at the head of the queue. He was a large black guy in a flat cap that Cynthia recognised as one of the dudes from the top tier. A mortified Tyler, for that was the pilot's actual name, looked to his crotch to find that his flies were not, in fact, undone. A lazy laugh rippled along the assembled commuters.

"Looks like someone's gonna be walking home," Tyler said.

"Get your Aryan jawbone outta my way," said the wit as he boarded the plane. "Some of us got real work to do."

Twice a day this plane, which had the SpaceWurd logo emblazoned on the tail and looked like it had just arrived from the future, made the twenty-minute hop back and forth to the spaceport which was sandwiched between the Coconino National Forest and Grand Canyon National Park. Despite the lack of commercial space flights thus far, take-offs and landings were frequent what with this airborne taxi service and the night-time test flights, which Gene back on his hot dog trailer held accountable for the spate of UFO sightings across the region.

"You're seeing lights in the sky. Over yonder is a spaceport. Do the frickin' math, genius," he'd say with eyes narrowed.

Cynthia slipped off her leather jacket, dumped her shoulder bag and took a seat. No one came to sit next to her, for which she was grateful. She didn't think it was worth bringing anything to read for such a short flight time, so instead, as she ate, she played a game on her cell.

After no time at all, the pilot with the Aryan jawbone came on speaker. "Ladies and gentlemen. This is Captain Buck Rogers speaking. We will shortly be touching down at blah blah blah so you know the drill."

The passengers, about thirty in all, dutifully put their devices and magazines away and buckled up.

If anything, it was chillier here than it was back at Scottsdale. This didn't bother Cynthia, though, as she disembarked with her jacket slung over shoulder. She took a moment to admire the scenery, which never fell short of breathtaking. The spaceport was situated in a wide expanse of flat land flanked by distant forests on one side and rocky plateaus on the other. She cut a glance over at the vast hangar on the port's northern rim, tantalisingly out of bounds for all but authorised personnel. Housed within was Astraeus 1 and Astraeus 2, the sum total of the company's space fleet thus far.

As the gabble of evening commuters approached the gleaming chrome and glass building which would have looked equally at home on Mars, a tired-looking bunch of early-shifters came plodding out, keen to get on board that damn plane and go home.

Jeez, Cynthia thought, *is that how I look when I walk*

out of here?

She and her colleagues nodded their hellos as they passed, and as she entered the building one of the security guys eyed her up and down. Cynthia cut quite a figure, with her blonde mohawk, horn-rimmed glasses, multiple ear piercings, shredded jeans and combat boots.

"Haven't you run out of room yet?" the security guy asked, nodding towards the cascade of tattoos spilling from the sleeves of her Butcher Babies t-shirt.

"Nah. Still got plenty of real estate left."

She fumbled around in her shoulder bag for her SmartCard, zapped herself in on the little black box on the wall and headed for the elevator.

Cynthia loved the reaction she got when she told people she worked at the SpaceWurd spaceport. If they weren't interested in her before, they sure as hell were now. Their eyes would light up and all of a sudden they'd be full of questions: *Have you had a ride in the Astraeus? Have you ever met the boss man? Are you going to go into space?* And inevitably: *So what do you do?*

She also, in equal measure, revelled in the reaction she got when she answered this last one: "Oh, I monitor emergency entrances and exits."

She got a perverse kick out of disappointing people. Always had done, always would do. It was probably why she was so good at it. It would also explain why she was still basically on the bottom rung of her particular career ladder, despite being whip smart.

The elevator door opened and Cynthia, along with about half a dozen others, tumbled into SpaceWurd's International Monitoring Station. Cynthia was looking forward to the day when that would become SpaceWurd's Intergalactic Monitoring Station, and she would have to watch over entrances and exits on the moon. But that was a while off yet.

She parked her butt in a chair in front of a bank of monitors and logged in. As the screens flickered into life she pulled a bottle of water out of her bag and placed it on the desk next to the keyboard. Then she pulled out her lucky action figure – 'The Thing' from *The Fantastic Four*, for whom she'd always had a soft spot – and positioned him on the other side.

"It's clobberin' time," she whispered.

For the final part of her daily ritual, she fished her MP3 player out of her bag (phones were strictly verbatim), plugged in and hit the button. As the heavy metal bounce of Sumo Cyco filled her ears, Cynthia settled in for a long, uneventful night of staring at doors.

Or so she thought.

Time did not exist in this particular workplace. As it was below ground there were no windows through which you could idly gaze out at the day, or the night. The passing of the sun or the moon ceased to matter. There was just you and others like you sitting at workstations, staring at screens.

SpaceWurd had about a dozen sites around the world,

including the Arizona spaceport, and it was from this spot that they were all monitored via CCTV. It could be midnight here in Arizona, but the view on your monitor could be of a security door at their lab off the east coast of Africa, in which case it was 10 o'clock in the morning. It was very discombobulating.

Cynthia had completely lost track of time when a big, steaming pile of you-know-what suddenly hit the fan. Her boredom-induced stupor had long since set in, robbing her of her mental acuity, and all she knew was that there was movement. Lots of it. There were people rushing around, coming in, leaving again, huddling around monitors and arguing in frantic whispers. She pulled her earbuds out and realised all this movement was accompanied by a heck of a lot of noise. Whatever this was, it was serious.

She leaned over to her friend at the next workstation. "Hey, Matt, what's going on? Somebody order the wrong flavour pizza?"

"Feeched if I know," Matt replied, leaning in close. "Way above our pay grade, though. That's for sure. This is top tier."

The top tier was, conversely, the name given to the lowest level in the spaceport complex. The site had been built upside down, with only the departures and arrivals suites above ground. Everything else was below the earth, and the deeper you went the more high-ranking the people you met. The top tier was where SpaceWurd's Central Security control room was situated. Cynthia had never had cause to be summoned down that far. Yet.

The monitoring station was on full alert now, but nobody had the slightest idea why. The place was buzzing with chatter, and rumours and theories were bouncing off the walls: *I hear Mr B himself is flying in. I think there's been another crash. It's a terrorist threat, you'll see.* And on and on it went.

Finally, a scrap of clarity was offered up to the monitoring station workers and everyone was called into the very well-appointed boardroom. Cynthia elbowed her way through her colleagues to grab a much sough-after seat.

"If I can have some quiet, please," hollered their supervisor, Ed.

Cynthia, and probably everyone else in the room too, smirked as they watched Ed wring his hands and shift from one foot to the other. This was something he always did when in the presence of one of his superiors.

Ed began, "You've probably all become aware that something has happened. It's nothing for us to worry about, obviously, but as monitors there are things we need to be made aware of. This is Neal Terry from the top…erm…from Central Security."

Cynthia recognised the wit from the plane earlier that evening. She couldn't help noticing that he was still wearing his flat cap. He was also brandishing a coffee cup from which steam was wafting. The expression on his face suggested he was the kind of man who never got excited about anything, ever. A real seen-it-all-done-it-all type.

"Thank you, Ed," said this Neal Terry guy. He appeared to stare hard at Ed from the corners of his eyes for a moment, as if discreetly studying him. Then he addressed the throng with a sigh, "If the research laboratory off the East Africa coast is in your remit…"

Cynthia's ears pricked up.

"…then this concerns you. What I'm about to tell you is going to sound pretty far-fetched, but I ain't one for yanking peoples' chains so you'd better listen close and hard. I might also add that everything that's about to spill out of my pretty mouth is highly confidential, so don't go sticking it on Facebook or whatever the hell else people your age do. Got that?"

A half-hearted murmur of understanding rippled around the room. Despite this, Neal knew that at least half the people here would be sharing this news with the entire planet the second they clocked out. Indeed, Cynthia was already making plans to meet her friends and tell them everything she was about to hear.

Chapter 2

The boat hit shore at 09:27 EAT. That's 11:27 MST or 06.27 GMT. We can be exact on this because it was picked up by the perimeter cameras. It was an old open lifeboat, navy blue, and we counted seven people on board. Eight if you want to include the baby.

There were two young women, probably around 22-25 years of age. Looked like sisters. It was one of these that had the baby. Then there was a middle-aged guy and an older woman. He was late 30s, early 40s. Her, pushing 70. We think they were mother and son. There were two boys, both looked the same age, maybe 18. And lastly there was the guy with the Kalashnikov.

He was obviously crew. He had the rest of them drag the boat up off the beach and into the trees. Obviously didn't want to be seen. We surmised the passengers were refugees and he was one of the pirates they'd paid to smuggle them to wherever they were going. Anyway, their timing sucked, because they did this right when Cyclone Ava was battering the hell out of Madagascar. Bad idea.

The US navy has an FSF-1 permanently patrolling these waters, so we tipped them off and as soon as the weather eased they went in to see if there was anything left of the ship. There wasn't. Just debris and bodies. By that time, of course, the lifeboat was well away. Mr B apparently had a quick pow-wow with the g-men and the decision was made to let it make landfall. Most of the passengers didn't survive more than ten minutes.

Journal entry dated 7th Jan 2018

***

"So what do we do now?" asked one of the boys.

Despite the fact he was brandishing an assault rifle, Mohamud, who was still young himself, probably no more than twenty-five, looked like a cornered deer. "I don't know," he stammered.

Esperance was having none of that. "You're not allowed to not know," she snapped. "We paid you to get us to South Africa. You have to have a back-up plan."

"Smuggling people over borders doesn't come with insurance," Mohamud retorted.

"So is that your way of saying no one's coming looking for us?"

"You're refugees. I'm a pirate. Of course no one's coming looking for us. We're on our own, unless we can attract attention from a passing ship."

"That's not good enough," said Godriva. "I've got a

baby to look after. We can't just wait. He has needs."

Godriva suddenly felt hopelessly exposed on her baby's behalf. She snuggled Bukeneza, Buki for short, up under her chin, rocking him to keep him from crying. He was looking eagerly around at these exciting new surroundings, blissfully unaware of the desperate situation he was in.

When the ship had gone down in the deep underworld of the night, all Godriva had manage to salvage was the small backpack containing baby supplies she now wore on her back. That and the light dress she had been wearing when the wave had hit. She suddenly remembered that she still had her phone. She handed Buki to her sister, slipped off the backpack and fished it out of the pocket on the side. No signal. Others checked theirs. Same result.

Esperance returned Buki and checked her own phone. With a roll of her eyes she slipped it back into the pocket of her shorts. She had managed to escape the capsizing ship with nothing but those and a vest. She'd even had to ditch her rucksack with the supplies for herself and her younger sister. She had not been allowed to bring it onto the lifeboat as it was too big.

"Do you even know where we are?" Godriva asked, not yet ready to let this Mohamud guy off the hook. "Is this Madagascar?"

"No. We didn't get that far. Wherever this is, it's north of Madagascar."

"If I might interject," said Leonce, the middle-aged

man who was accompanied by his mother. "If rescue does come, you really don't want to be caught waving that thing about." He nodded towards Mohamud's assault rifle. "Maybe you should get rid of it."

Mohamud raised the gun, Terminator-style. "Nice try," he smirked.

Leonce rolled his eyes. "Oh, for goodness' sake! What do you think we're going to do? Mutiny? If rescue comes and you're seen with a gun, they might just sail off and leave us here!"

"Or start shooting," Esperance added.

"The gun stays."

Godriva snorted with derision. "It's because of people like you that we fled Burundi in the first place."

"That's not my problem."

"It is now."

"Maybe we should start a fire on the beach, to attract attention," suggested one of the boys, whose name was Vital. He was obviously keen to diffuse the conversation.

"Yeah," said the other kid, Walter. "Maybe we'll be spotted by a plane or something. We could say we're tourists heading for Madagascar, or…"

"Tourists, huh?" snickered Mohamud. "So where are your passports?"

Throughout this exchange, the older woman, Yanka, had remained silent, until now. "Shush," she said. "Can anyone else hear something?"

The talking ceased. Everyone tilted their heads to try

14

and listen beyond the surface noise of waves lapping against shore, breeze blowing through trees, birds cawing. There was something there alright, and it sounded like...yelling?

The party of seven, eight if you want to include the baby, broke from their tree cover and stepped cautiously out onto the beach. The wind was fresh and cool, as it usually is after a storm, and it carried the noise their way.

"Over there," said Yanka, pointing towards the headland.

It was early and the sun was still low in the sky. Framed against it was a pack of men. They were charging towards the shipwrecked survivors, scattering the seabirds that dotted the beach as they neared. 'Pack' is the word that presented itself to Esperance because they seemed more like wild animals than people; sprinting, screaming, roaring, grimacing. She quickly counted ten of them, all freakishly tall, completely naked, utterly hairless and...

"There're blue," said Leonce.

"Can't be," said Esperance, still squinting into the morning glare.

"They are," said Walter. "They really are blue."

"They must be like...seven-foot tall, or something," Vital added.

None of the survivors moved, mostly because they did not know how to respond to a sight as bizarre as this. They were being charged by a pack of naked, blue-skinned giants with penises swinging wildly and faces contorted into visages of rage. But as the pack neared, their bloodlust became impossible to deny.

Godriva was the first to break. "Run," she simply said.

And run they did.

The party scattered. Holding her baby boy tightly against her chest, Godriva made for the trees. Esperance followed as shouting and gunfire erupted behind her. She put herself between the gunfire and her sister with her baby. Even with her son in her arms, Godriva sprinted like a pro athlete; light, lithe and fast. With her identical physique, Esperance kept pace easily. She looked back over her shoulder to see Yanka going down under the pack of blue men in a frenzy of blood and limbs. There was a kind of cool fascination to it, like watching a pride of lions taking down a zebra on a nature doc. Yanka's son swung punches and kicks in a desperate attempt to save his mother but he lasted only seconds. He died with teeth in his throat.

"Don't stop!" gasped Esperance. "For god's sake don't stop!"

Again there was the rapid rat-a-tat of bullets leaving barrel followed by screaming. Mohamud was down. Three of the blue savages broke from the pack and zeroed in on Esperance and Godriva.

"RUUUUN!" screamed Esperance. "RUUUUUUN!"

They broke out into the open, an expanse of ground and sparse grass riddled with pools of rainwater from the destructive storm of the previous night. Beyond this expanse was a rocky outcrop.

"That way! Head for the rocks!"

"I can't climb with Buki," Godriva gasped.

"You'll have to!"

Esperance risked a peek behind. The three blues had now broken tree cover and were closing. "What are they?" she yelled.

Across the plain she saw the two boys sprinting away with a pair of the blue savages in close pursuit. They were fast though, the boys, and they looked like they might make it. Then Godriva reached the wall of rock. By now little Buki was howling.

"Climb!" shouted Esperance as she pushed her sister up by the backside. "Just climb!"

Godriva scrambled upwards as best she could with just one free arm. As her feet searched for purchase she sent a small avalanche of grit and pebbles down onto Esperance who had started following. She had cleared head height by the time the fastest of the blues hit the stone wall. With long limbs grasping wildly, he began ascending faster than seemed humanly possible. There was blood around his mouth and running down his neck and chest. Esperance screamed and kicked at his head.

"Look out!" came a cry from above.

Esperance looked up to see her sister standing on the precipice with a rock held high above her head. She flattened herself against the stone wall as the rock whizzed past. It connected with the blue man's face and sent him crashing down onto his two fellow savages. Esperance reached the outcrop's plateau and was hauled to her feet by her sister. Buki was on the ground, wailing. Below them, the blue man who had been struck by the rock whimpered and yelped as he pawed at what was left of his face. The other two circled and growled.

"They are like lions," said Esperance.

"Or sharks," Godriva offered.

Esperance jogged over to the opposite side of the outcrop and from her vantage point peered through the soft morning haze. If it wasn't for the fact she and Godriva were being hunted by a pack of frenzied blue giants who wanted to rip them to pieces, she might have said it was a beautiful day. In the distance, bleached by the low sunlight, she spotted a scattering of buildings enclosed by a high fence.

"Look. Over there. A compound!"

Dominating the compound, and easily visible from the sisters' vantage point, was a huge dome and a large satellite dish, its feed horn pointing up at the sky.

"What is it?" Godriva pondered as she picked up her crying baby. "A military base?"

"Could be. They can help us. Come on."

Godriva paused. "Is that wise? We're refugees. Won't they just arrest us and…?"

"Better that than ending up as breakfast for those…things."

Esperance looked back down at the three blue men who had pursued them. The injured one was still there,

18

quivering and whimpering, but the other two were running off.

"Where are they going?"

"No idea. They might be heading around the long way. We're not going to survive if we stay out here. That base is our only chance. We've got to move."

Esperance took the lead and scrambled down the rocky wall on the far side. The surface was dry and crumbly, giving way easily beneath her feet and fingertips. She slid down the last few feet and landed in an undignified heap on her backside.

"Ow! Now you."

"But Buki…"

Esperance reached up. "Pass him down to me."

Godriva gingerly lowered herself down as far as she could by gripping onto a rock at the top. Then she reached down and handed the child to her sister. As she did so her grip gave way. Esperance jumped clear as Godriva hit the ground hard, shoulder first.

"Godriva!"

Esperance gently placed the sobbing, frightened baby onto the ground and squatted by her sister, telling her not to move.

"My arm," Godriva winced. "My arm, it's…broken." The pain jabbing through it was fearsome.

"Shush," said Esperance. "Let me see."

Esperance snapped into nurse-mode, for that was her profession. She helped Godriva up into a sitting position against the wall of rock, her sister gritting her teeth the whole time. She noticed that Godriva's right shoulder was now at a ninety-degree angle to her neck and that her arm was internally rotated.

"Can you touch your other shoulder?"

"No," Godriva gasped, her face scrunched up in agony. "I can barely move it."

Esperance then started tickling the palm and fingertips of her sister's right hand.

"Can you feel that?"

"Yes."

"Good. I'm just going to check the deltoid area of your shoulder. This may hurt."

It did, and Godriva jolted as barbs of pain crackled through her nerve endings.

"Ah! Ow! Ow! Stop!"

"Not broken," said Esperance. "Just dislocated. In normal circumstances, we'd put this back in under sedation. I can do it for you now but it's going to be agony. Are you ready?"

Godriva wasn't, and so she tried stalling. "Where's Buki?"

"He's here. Look."

Esperance moved aside so that Godriva could see her baby who had been safely laid on the ground.

"Hey, Buki," breathed Godriva. "Hey there, baby boy. Baby boy…"

Esperance watched in fascination as Godriva's expression slowly changed from one of endless love to one of pure horror.

"They're…they're…" panted Godriva.

"What is it, sister?"

"They're back!"

Esperance followed Godriva's line of vision and saw two of the blue-skinned giants clearing the far end of the rocky outcrop. Even from this distance, she could tell they were moving lightning-fast.

"Come on!" snapped Esperance.

She grabbed hold of Godriva's good arm and helped her up. Godriva yelped in pain.

"Our only hope is that base!"

"But my arm!"

"Hold it as firmly as you can against your side with your other arm. I'll take Buki."

Esperance scooped the child up off the ground and began running, her sister beside her. However, Godriva was much slower now because of her injury. Every footstep sent a jab of electrical pain coursing up her arm, through her shoulder and into her neck. The base was only about a kilometre away but might as well have been fifty.

"Not going to make it," croaked Godriva, her throat burning.

"We have to."

Buki watched in stunned silence as this new world whizzed by in a blur of muted colours and painful noise. He would have cried were it not for the constant bump-bump-bump of his aunt's sprinting footsteps, which he found mesmerising.

Esperance looked back and saw that the two blues were closing fast. And then the ground vanished from beneath her feet. As she plummeted, free-falling in slow-motion, she heard the sound of her sister's voice yelling, "BUUUUUKIIIII!"

Esperance's feet connected with the ground and she allowed herself to go with the momentum, completing a perfect forward roll before springing back up into a standing position with Buki still in her arms.

"Is he okay?" a frantic Godriva asked.

Buki looked up at his mother, who was standing over them both, and laughed.

"I don't think he even noticed," Esperance said. "What just happened?"

"You're in a trench. It leads to the base. I think it might go under the fence."

"Then let's go."

Godriva unceremoniously dumped her behind down onto the trench's edge and then pushed herself off with her feet, landing roughly and painfully.

"OOOOOWWWWW!"

"We must hurry," Esperance said, as if Godriva needed reminding.

Esperance launched off at a sprint with Godriva lagging sorely behind. As they progressed, the trench became deeper and the walls became higher until they were below ground level. Somewhere behind, the two blue savages crashed down into the trench and rampaged after them, gnashing their teeth and growling.

And then all became dark. The trench had become a tunnel.

"I can see lights up ahead!" Godriva panted.

The tunnel had solid flooring which, if nothing else, made the running easier. Also, there was track lighting built into the floor and the ceiling; green lights below, white lights above.

"Not much further!" Esperance yelled back over her shoulder.

Godriva said nothing. She just ran as best she could while cradling her bad arm. She looked behind and... "THEY'RE GAINING!" she screamed.

Like wild animals with the scent of prey, the blues were closing the gap.

"I can see a dead end!" yelled Esperance. "Oh, please god, no!"

Sensing her terror, Buki started to cry.

"It's a door!"

Godriva was right, it was a door, flat and round and made of solid steel with no apparent mechanism for opening it.

"Now what?" Godriva panted.

"There's a control panel!" Esperance yelped. "Press something!"

To the top right of the huge steel door was a numbered keypad.

"What shall I press?" Godriva pleaded.

"Anything! They're almost on us!"

The two blues were far too tall for the tunnel and

were now approaching on all fours, like jackals, which was slowing them down. Godriva released her injured arm and with her left hand jabbed hopelessly at the keypad. She and Esperance knew there was no way on god's green earth that she was going to, by sheer chance, hit the right combination of numbers to open the door, but neither of them were ready to die. Also, neither of them wanted to contemplate the horror of Buki's life being snuffed out when it had barely begun. They would cling onto their lives until the bitter end.

And then something miraculous happened. From inside the door came the sound of a powerful mechanism unlocking. With a hiss it began to open away from the two sisters, who could only look to each other in wide-eyed amazement.

"What did you press?" Esperance asked.

"I have no idea!"

"Never mind! Go!"

Godriva slithered through the gap. The door was still moving and she couldn't help noticing that it was at least a foot thick. Esperance followed behind. The blues were close now, perhaps only twenty feet away, and narrowing the gap swiftly. Their mouths were bloody and their teeth were bared, but their eyes, locked onto their prey, were cold and focused. As soon as Esperance was inside, the door changed direction and began to close, as if it knew the sisters were now safely within its protection. But it was moving agonisingly slowly and the blues were almost onto them. Godriva put her back to the door and started pushing.

"Help me," she said.

Esperance put a shoulder to it. However, their efforts made no difference. The door moved no quicker as the growling beyond it grew closer and louder.

"It's no good!"

A long blue arm whipped through the gap, grasping and clawing at Godriva, who was closest. She screamed as fingers found hair and clenched.

"GODRIVA!" Esperance screamed.

Godriva twisted and turned in a desperate effort to free herself, her right arm swinging stiffly and agonisingly. All Esperance could do with the baby still in her arms was look on and yell. Then the grip released and the arm disappeared. Its owner had snatched it back through the door at the last possible second. Somewhere inside that great slab of steel the mechanism locked into place, trapping the two young women inside and the blue horrors out.

Exhausted and disbelieving, all Godriva and Esperance could do was look to each other. Gradually, their panting died down.

"What were those…those *things*?" Esperance's face curled up in disgust as she said the word.

"I don't know. They were like wild animals. Like carnivores."

"Did you see what happened to the old lady and her son? They went for their throats. They ripped them to pieces."

"And the smuggler too. Fat load of good that gun did him in the end," said Godriva with a curl of the lip.

"I hope those boys got away."

"They were pretty fast. I'm sure they're okay. Maybe they'll find their way here."

The sisters studied the sanctuary they had found themselves in. It was sleek, white, brightly lit and completely silent. If the blue men were still outside in the tunnel, not a sound from them could be heard, which was reassuring. Opposite the tunnel door was another one, a larger one, with an oval window built into it.

"It's like an airlock," said Esperance.

"How do you know what an airlock looks like?"

"I've seen *Star Trek*."

Having had enough of being ignored despite his crying, Buki decided that a change of tact was in order, so he began to whimper pathetically.

"He's frightened," said Esperance. "Frightened and hungry."

"And probably needs changing," Godriva added.

Esperance held the wet, blubbery baby close and shushed him. As Buki dribbled onto her shoulder, she peered through the oval window in the airlock door, expecting to see soldiers, people, activity, but instead there was only darkness.

"Hm. Can't see a thing."

It was just as well.

There was a ladder leading up to a hatch in the ceiling high above.

"We're deeper than I thought," Esperance said. "Here. Take him."

She handed Buki to Godriva, who cradled him in her good arm, and then started to climb.

"Be careful," said Godriva.

Still functioning on pure adrenalin, Esperance reached the top of the ladder in mere seconds. There was a handle on the hatch and Esperance hoped to god it was a manual lock. She grabbed it and turned. It was indeed manual. She pushed the hatch up until it fell open, then she stuck her head out and peered around.

"We're inside the compound but it's deserted," she called down. "Come on up."

"You're going to have to come back down for Buki. I can't hold him and climb."

Esperance did so, and moments later the two sisters, along with the baby, were standing in the compound grounds under the hazy sunlight. Between them and the rest of the island was a stainless-steel fence at least twenty feet high and topped with razor wire.

"We're safe," said Esperance.

She couldn't have been more wrong.

Chapter 3

The commercial space flights division was the Wurd Corporation's latest venture after the search engine and the streaming service. Well, 'venture' was one word for it. Another might have been 'egotrip'.

The company had been founded back in the internet's dark ages (i.e. 1994) by one Byron Wurd. He had already made his fortune before entering the burgeoning online market, in toys. His chain of toyshops, Wurd's World, had gone international, but Mr B (as he was known to his employees) had very early on recognised the importance of data harvesting, and so he had invested in SEO technology. Needless to say, that had paid off big time, and still did. But now he wanted to take the Wurd brand into space, and so SpaceWurd (as in 'spaceward'), was born. But the prospect of taking a short trip outside the Earth's atmosphere was just the cover story, there to dazzle the media, attract the celebs and set the online forums buzzing. No, the real story was happening quite literally beneath the surface, in SpaceWurd's secret facility on a private island off the east coast of Africa, as Cynthia was now aware.

She did not listen to music the next day as she worked, if you could call what she did working. She was too on edge and didn't want to miss anything, should something else go down. Some of the things this Neal Terry guy had passed onto them the previous day were pretty freaky. It seemed there was a heck of a lot more going on at this company than Cynthia and her colleagues in monitoring had realised.

"You know what I'm thinking?" Cynthia whispered to Matt on the next workstation. "If that's the stuff they're prepared to tell us, what the hell *aren't* they prepared to tell us?"

"Yeah, good question," said Matt. "I always think that for every one thing these corporate suits disclose, there's at least six they don't."

"I gotta be honest," Cynthia added with not a little relish, "I used to think this job was duller than dishwater. Now I'm not so sure. I can't help wondering what's gonna happen next."

She wouldn't have to wait long to find out.

At the previous day's meeting the monitoring team had been told, in the sketchiest way possible and without surrendering too much detail, that an experiment had gone wrong at the laboratory and that the company had been forced to 'allow the test subjects beyond the facility perimeter'. Neal Terry's words.

Matt leaned in again. "Even 'Captain Buck Rogers' on the plane this morning looked like someone had

29

taken a leak on his breakfast bagel. Did you notice?"

"Yeah. Definitely not his usual exuberant self."

That had been the first of today's clues that the tentacles of this 'failed experiment' were groping their way through the company. The second was the amount of shifty looking men and women in dark suits they'd seen milling around the building after they'd clocked in.

"What do you think happened?" Matt asked.

Cynthia shrugged. "I never play the guessing game. Waste of time. You can hit on the right answer and not even know it, so what's the point? I'm prepared to wait until we either find out or we don't."

"Fair enough," said Matt. "But whatever it is, it's big."

"Yeah. I don't know about you, but every time something goes shit-shaped, my first thought is always that I'm gonna get laid off. Without me even being conscious of it, it's my biggest fear in life."

"S'alright for you," said Matt with a little smile. "You got no kids. Me on the other hand…"

Cynthia and Matt had known each other for years, having once upon a time played together in a band. Outsiders often assumed they were siblings as they seemed to come from the same primordial pool of cynicism and humour. But even without the sibling thing, they looked like they belonged to the same crowd, what with their penchants for tattoos, piercings, metal t-shirts and leather jackets.

Cynthia returned to her screens. Among the

30

entrances and exits she monitored were several at the East Africa lab in question, so she was in hyper alert-mode. The one she was looking at right now was a gloomy below-ground emergency door. She clicked her mouse and brought up another image: a service entrance in an underground staff car park in the New York office. What was it with this company and underground sites?

I thought they were trying to go up, not down, Cynthia thought. *No wonder their spaceships keep blowing up.*

Another click of the mouse brought up the airlock at the East Africa lab site, then the heavy-duty service elevator in the same place. Over the past few years Cynthia had seen a lot of very hi-tech equipment being loaded into it and taken down, and a lot of dirt being brought back out, but at the mo it was at surface level and nothing was happening. Cynthia was almost disappointed. Every time she clicked back to the lab site now she expected to see something freaky.

She clicked again and found herself at the rocket testing site in Florida. Not much of a view there, just a massive hangar door with a big towing vehicle parked outside and a couple of guys in hard hats hanging around. All quiet.

By the time Cynthia clicked back to the lab site's emergency below-ground door, she had drifted into that strange netherworld of boredom-induced contemplation that exists somewhere between Zen and Nirvana. As her mind was lazily exploring the many wonders of the cosmos, a movement on the screen caught her eye and she let out a loud yelp.

"What the hell?" said a startled Matt.

He jumped out of his seat and stood behind Cynthia, his bearded chin almost resting on her shoulder as he gawped at her screen. On it were two young black women, one in a summer dress holding her arm which looked injured, the other in vest and shorts and holding a baby. There was no audio but there didn't need to be for Cynthia and Matt to know that these two women were in fear for their lives.

"Jesus effing Christ," Cynthia breathed as she caught sight of two giant blue men, completely naked, that were rampaging on all fours towards the cornered women. "It's them! Two of the test subjects they told us about yesterday! I can't believe it!"

Out of professional habit, Cynthia's eyes flicked down to the left-hand corner of the screen. There was the little red dot which meant that yes, this was being recorded.

"What the feech did they do to them?" said Matt a little too loudly, attracting stares and glares from across the monitoring room. Since becoming a father he had replaced his fucks with an alternative f-word. 'Feech' he had picked up from the TV movie *Caravan of Courage: An Ewok Adventure*. As a big Star Wars fan, he liked the idea of dropping Ewok-related f-bombs.

The blue men were closing in and, despite the gloominess of the image, Cynthia could tell that their top priority wasn't to make friends. Remembering protocol, she hit the big black button in the middle of her desk phone, summoning her supervisor, Ed.

"Cynthia...?" said Matt with huge of dollop of uncertainty.

The test subjects were almost onto the two women now. One of them, the girl in the summer dress with her eyes almost popping out of their sockets in terror, started jabbing at the door's keypad. Damning protocol to hell, Cynthia clicked her mouse and ordered the door to open. A small crowd had by now gathered around her, looking on as the two women and the baby slipped through the door. As soon as they were safely inside, Cynthia gave the order for the door to close again, hopefully in time to slam in the blue guys' faces. It was close, but there was no cigar as one of these blue savages got an arm through. Cynthia clicked the mouse and the POV changed to the airlock inside, and the assembled monitoring staff all held their breaths as the drama played out in brittle silence on the screen in front of them. The two women, one still clutching the baby, were trying to push the door shut as the long blue arm grasped and groped. It caught hold of one of the women, the one with the injured arm, by the hair. She screamed and cried as she tried to struggle free, but here in Arizona, on the other side of the world, no one could hear her.

The audience winced as the door tightened on the blue giant's arm, expecting to see it severed at the shoulder at any moment. But at the last possible second it disappeared back through the door. Cynthia clicked back to the POV in the gloomy tunnel to see the two blue men pounding and clawing at the now safely closed door. In their frustration, they then started jumping up and down and pounding their fists on the ground. They were also very obviously shrieking and hollering, but their cries were in vain.

"Well, this is all very interesting," said Matt drily.

"Like a couple of angry chimpanzees," Cynthia added.

After about a minute-and-a-half of going crazy, the blue men seemed to tire and then they both sloped off. Cynthia clicked back to the airlock to see one of the women climbing the ladder and disappearing from shot. They were safe. Cynthia looked nervously over her shoulder in time to see the parting of the crowd. In the gap left behind Ed appeared, and he did not look happy.

"What the hell have you just done?" was all he had to say.

Chapter 4

Vital and Walter clocked the two attractive sisters moments after stepping onto the ship for South Africa. Vital nudged his friend in the ribs.

"The one in the little shorts for me," he said. "You can have the one with the baby."

Like Esperance and Godriva, they too were escaping Burundi. But then, so were a lot of people at the time. They were fleeing to avoid recruitment into the feared Imbonerakure youth militia. Political dogma and violence held nothing but dread for them. Their hearts and minds belonged to football.

Friends since childhood, they had bonded over a shared love of Manchester United. Their younger days had been spent on a playing field on the outskirts of their hometown of Cankuzo, perfecting their headers, refining their tackling, improving their aim. Their latter days had been devoted to earning money to pay for football gear and tickets to matches, mostly by facilitating tourists in the safari park. Their ultimate dream was to make it all the way to the UK to play football professionally. This was where, after all, players were worshipped like gods, paid eye-watering sums of money and drove Ferraris. Of the harsh realities that awaited them they were blissfully ignorant.

They were both eighteen which was a dangerous age; old enough to act on their crazy plans and schemes but young enough to misread danger for adventure. And unfortunately for them adventure had come knocking mere hours after the ship, a long liner called 'Dream Angus' that resolutely failed to live up to its categorisation, had left dock.

"Head for that building!" Vital shouted. "For god's sake don't stop!"

Walter was crying as he sprinted, "I don't want to die! I don't want to die! I don't want to die!"

"Don't talk! Just run!"

The ground was riddled with pools of rainwater and the grass was long and sparse. In the clumps where it grew it came up to the boys' waists and acted as a drag, slowing them down. At an average of seven feet tall, however, the blue men pursuing them faced no such handicap. The grass did not even register with them. Also, they seemed to feel no pain despite running barefoot. They had the focused minds and singular vision of predators after prey.

"They're gaining!" Vital yelled.

Ahead, shimmering through the morning haze, was a collection of buildings. Even from this distance, it was obvious to Vital and Walter that these buildings were abandoned, what with them looking so dilapidated. Vital could actually see the rising sun through the roof of the largest of them. Great sections of that roof had in fact been ripped off by the storm of the previous night.

"If we can make it inside, we may be able to lose them!"

"I don't want to die! I don't want to die!" Walter cried as he splashed through a pool.

"You're not going to die! Just keep running!"

Vital had too much living to do to accept that death might already have caught up with him. He had spent too much time dreaming of the goals he had yet to score, of the women he had yet to love. He thought of the attractive sisters from the ship. He estimated them to be around five years or so older than himself and his friend. At the time that had seemed like an insurmountable obstacle, but now it registered as nothing more than a piffling little detail. And then they had all ended up in the same lifeboat.

It must be fate, he had thought.

But look what fate had dealt him now. He had earlier spotted the two sisters with babe in arms fleeing for their lives across the plain, just as he and Walter were now doing.

Not them! his inner voice had implored. *They are too beautiful to die!*

And then he had seen the one carrying the baby disappear. Literally vanish into thin air! It had sent his mind reeling, his reason nose-diving. Tribes of blue savages! Women disappearing! *What kind of nightmare island have we washed up on?*

"Not going to make it!" Walter panted.

"Not far now!" Vital urged. "We can make it!"

"I don't want to die!"

Perhaps Walter had not devoted as much time as Vital to laying down plans for his future. Perhaps he had been neglecting his stamina in training. Perhaps his grip on life was not as strong. Or perhaps, just perhaps, he had simply tripped. Either way, he went down in a flurry of limbs and a splash of water, leaving Vital to face the most difficult decision of his life: do I stop and help or do I keep running?

As a young boy, Vital would often find himself on the receiving end of good-natured advice from his gentle grandfather. One of those pieces of advice had been imparted to him more often than any other, and that was: "When in doubt, do the right thing."

Sometimes his grandfather, while making a jug of his famous mango lassi, would expand on this: "Throughout your life you will face dilemmas, decisions, forks in the road. Some of them will be very difficult indeed. Some of them may seem impossible. But deep down in your heart you will *always* know what the *right* thing to do is. So that's what you must do, no matter what. Always do the *right* thing and you can't go wrong."

In this case, the right thing to do was perfectly clear, even if it meant putting his own life in danger. Vital skidded to a halt and helped his friend. He pulled Walter, who looked stunned and shaken, to his feet.

"Come on, Walter. We're nearly there."

The blue giants were getting dangerously close now, but Walter's eyes were vacant.

"Can't run anymore."

"Walter! You have to! We can make it! It's just there! We can do it!" He pointed towards the ruined buildings.

"I'm done. You go. I'm done."

Vital felt a pit of anger boiling up inside him. "No! You can't make me do this! You can't make me leave you! We're supposed to be friends! We stick together, no matter what!"

"You go. It's hopeless, all of it. I'm done."

With tears streaming down his hot face, Vital began to back away, putting distance between himself and Walter. Beyond his friend, the blue savages, with bloodlust in their yellow eyes, were approaching fast in a cloud of dust.

Then Walter uttered his last words. "Give those sisters my love."

Angry, hurt, desperate, distraught, terrified and out of time, Vital turned and left his friend to his fate. The savages converged on Walter in a frenzy of teeth and nails. It was over in seconds. Vital did not – could not – look back.

It was clear that this place, whatever it was, had been abandoned for a few years at least. As he sprinted past

39

the outhouses, as light and as fast as a gazelle, Vital clocked a jeep, a bulldozer, several diggers and a sentry gate, all in ruin and overgrown with creepers. He made it to the building he had seen from the plain, the one the morning sunlight had been shining through. It promised plenty of places to hide, and birds flapped and cawed nervously as he entered.

It had once been a warehouse or storage facility, that much was obvious. The ground level was vast and open, but it had been reclaimed by the island and was now well on its way to becoming a natural habitat. Vital knew he might have no more than a minute or two to find somewhere to hide, so he headed up the metal steps, hoping they would not collapse under him. They didn't, but his trainers made a *tinktinktinktinktink* sound as he went.

The upper floor was more promising. There was junk everywhere; a pile of old tyres, storage crates, all open and empty, engine parts, and even a rusted motorbike well past its useful days. Also, there were compartments, cubicles. Perhaps there had once been offices here. Maybe he could hide out in one of...

A sound from below froze him. Could it have been those birds? Could it have been one of *them?* A large section of the floor was open and so he peered down. All was quiet again now. Nothing moved. He looked up and saw his shadow on the far wall. There was something not quite right about it. Despite the fact he was standing still, it was moving, and – no, his eyes were not deceiving him – getting bigger. It was the shadow of someone running. He turned to see a blue giant, silhouetted against the sun, sprinting at him. The blue man lunged and Vital ducked. He looked up and once again found himself alone. No blue man.

Vital edged over to the large, square, open section of the floor and looked down. The blue man was lying sprawled on the cement ground below. Was he dead? No, he was still moving, but now he was vulnerable. Vital looked around for something he could use as a weapon to finish the blue monstrosity off. The motorbike! He could push it over the edge and onto his attacker. He ran over to it, heaved it upright by the handlebars and pushed. It was heavy but it was moving. Just as he was building momentum it stopped with a jolt. There were creepers wrapped around the frame and they had become ensnared in the back wheel. He let the bike drop, which it did with a massive clang, and started ripping the creepers away with his bare hands. Before picking the bike up again he risked a peek over the edge. The blue savage was gone.

He held his breath and listened. The only sound to be heard was the gentle wind from outside. No footsteps. No running. Even the birds had fallen silent. He looked up and saw his shadow on the far wall. There was something not quite right about it.

You are kidding me, he thought.

He inhaled sharply, wheeled around and saw the same blue giant sprinting at him from out of the sun.

Again he ducked and the blue man disappeared.

Surely not, Vital thought.

He peered over the edge to see his would-be attacker sprawled over the floor. Again. This time Vital did not hesitate. He grabbed the motorbike and ran with it. It went tumbling over the precipice, its full weight crashing down onto Vital's would-be attacker. *Now* he was dead.

"That's for Walter, you big blue bastard!" Vital cried.

Chapter 5

"When's this going to end?" Godriva was crying, shaking, inconsolable. "When's this going to end? There's no way out! No way out!"

Esperance grasped Godriva's face in her hands, forcing her sister to look at her. "You have to be strong," she urged. "You have to be strong for Buki. He needs his mother."

After emerging from the hatch within the compound they had lucked straight into what seemed to be the site's living quarters. When safely inside they had locked themselves in a bunkroom.

"This isn't going end! This is our lives now! We're never going to make it to Durban!"

"So, what are you saying?" Esperance snapped back. "That we should have stayed in Bujumbura?"

"No! Burundi is dead to me now! I can never go back!"

For Godriva, Burundi had died along with Benjamin, her lover. He was a porter at the hospital where Esperance was a nurse. It was she who had introduced him to Godriva. Benjamin was a sweet and gentle young man, very old fashioned in his ways. When not in work he always wore a pressed shirt and a bow tie. He lived with his grandmother and took care of her, and with the little money he had bought Godriva flowers and chocolates.

When Godriva had learned she was expecting, she felt as though she'd been cast adrift in a flimsy boat on a stormy ocean. The hands of Benjamin became her anchors, but it was her sister's hands that had held onto hers the day Bukeneza came into the world.

One Saturday afternoon, Benjamin happened to be in the wrong place at the wrong time and was set upon by an Imbonerakure gang. They beat him to the ground with sticks and proceeded to use his head as a football, all while two police officers looked on. He was taken to the hospital where it took him four days to die. Esperance was his nurse. He never got to see his son.

"This is no place to raise a baby," Godriva had afterwards announced. "I am going."

"To where?"

"I have friends in South Africa. If I can get there, they can help me start a new life with my Buki."

"But what will you do?"

"Wherever you go in the world, they will always need schoolteachers."

"And nurses," Esperance had added.

By turning her back on the country that had caused her so much pain, Godriva felt the satisfying pang of retribution, as if Burundi itself would sit and cry in the dark after she'd gone, smarting from its abandonment.

And while Godriva wanted to keep her baby safe from the youth militia gangs, Esperance wanted to keep her sister safe from the world, and so they had fled together. They, along with a great tide of others just like them, had made the long, hot journey across Tanzania by road before crossing the border into Kenya to seek sea passage from Mombasa.

"This island is cursed. It's unnatural. We're going to die here," Godriva moaned.

"Dying is a choice," Esperance said firmly. "If you decide you're going to die, then you will. I've decided I'm going to live."

"Benjamin didn't have a choice."

Godriva stroked Buki's tiny face. He was a small part of Benjamin that still lived.

"No," Esperance conceded. "He didn't, but we do. We're safe in here."

There would be no way for the blue savages to surmount the perimeter fence, which was just as well because four of them had been pacing back and forth beyond it since the pursuit had ended. And the living block where Esperance and Godriva had found sanctuary was a two-storey building with a door that locked from the inside. The bunkrooms they had discovered in an upper-floor corridor also locked from the inside.

"Where is everyone?" Godriva pondered aloud. "It's

so strange that there's no one here."

"I have no idea. It is very weird."

It had been the first thing they noticed after emerging from the hatch within the compound: no people.

"The place still looks occupied," Esperance continued. "Some of the bunkrooms still have belongings in them. I just don't understand it."

"It's creepy," Godriva added. "It's like everyone just vanished. Poof!"

"Hm. How is your shoulder now?"

Godriva's shoulder was still at a funny angle and her right arm turned inward.

"It hurts."

"I'm going to see if I can find any medical supplies."

"Be careful. And don't be too long," said Godriva sullenly.

"I'll just be a couple of minutes. Lock the door behind me."

Twenty minutes later, Esperance returned.

"Where have you been?" an angry Godriva demanded. "I thought something had happened!"

"I've been looking all over. There really is no one here. It's so strange. None of those blue things either, thank god. Except for the ones outside, but they can't get in so that's okay. But the good news is we've got everything we need to keep us going for months if need be; food, water, and this…" She held aloft a large first aid kit. "There's a whole medical bay downstairs. Very hi-tech. In fact, everything is. This place is state-of-the-art."

Godriva visibly relaxed a little. Buki was lying on his back next to her on the bunk, happily gurgling to himself.

"Don't suppose you found any milk formula down there."

"No," Esperance replied. "No sign of a crèche either, so there were no children here."

"I can't understand how everyone could just disappear. And what are those blue…things outside?"

"I don't know. All I'm worried about now is your shoulder. There's morphine in here. I checked. Are you ready?"

"Will it hurt?"

"Not after a dose of this," said Esperance who was by now brandishing a syringe.

Having her shoulder pushed back into its socket did not hurt half as much as having the morphine injection. Once the deed was done, Esperance set Godriva's arm in a sling.

"Now that your arm is set, you have to come and see this," Esperance said. "I'll take Buki."

Buki was enjoying the relative peace inside his new surroundings. The rapid movement had stopped, and the shouting and screaming too. Everything seemed calm now, and just as he was starting to feel sleepy, he found himself scooped up by his aunt. Esperance led Godriva, who was still cradling her arm, out of the bunkroom, along the corridor, through a canteen area and up some stairs. She held a door open and Godriva stepped out.

The view from up here was indeed a beautiful one. Grey clouds were still rolling across the sky, the remnants of last night's storm, and Godriva watched as they sent great shadows tumbling across the plain.

"There are sun loungers, chairs, tables, parasols and potted plants downstairs," Esperance explained. "They must have brought them all inside ahead of the hurricane."

"Which means there could have been people here as recently as yesterday," Godriva added.

"Perhaps they had to evacuate because of the storm. Anyway, if I bring the chairs and tables and everything else back up, it means we can keep watch from up here. And look at that."

Protruding from the roof of the doorway was a pole, atop of which was affixed a CCTV camera and a loudspeaker.

"Are we being watched?" asked a shocked Godriva.

Esperance shook her head. "I don't think so. There's a few of them throughout the site but I think they're all dead. I didn't see any of them move and there's no little red lights on any of them, like the ones back at the hospital."

Godriva waved at the camera with her good arm. "Hello. Hello," she said feebly.

"I think you're wasting your time," said Esperance with a shrug. She was right.

Godriva scanned the horizon, the limits of their

brand-new world. A hill of earth swept upwards towards the heavens and back down again, meeting a thick tangle of trees from where drifted the distant cawing of birds. The trees gave way to a long stretch of beach, the ocean beyond it as still and silent as glass. The sea imbued the air with a salty freshness, which was revitalising and welcome. Godriva could see the plain of dust and wild grass they had fled across earlier, and the rocky outcrop from which she had fallen.

And then there was the compound itself; a sprawling network of low-level buildings enclosed by a high, strong, steel fence. Glinting in the sun was the dome. It was a metallic structure, large and imposing.

"I wonder what's under there," Esperance said.

"Perhaps we are better off not knowing, sister."

Next to the dome was the big satellite dish that Esperance and Godriva had spotted from the rocky outcrop. It was housed on top of a squat, concrete building along with various other dishes and antennas.

"What do you think that's for?" Godriva asked, nodding towards it.

"I don't know but I've never seen a dish that big before, except in the movies. That must be a communications room, I suppose. Hopefully we'll be able to get word out, call for help. Oh, and have you noticed there's no way in or out?"

"What? No gate or…?"

"No. Nothing. Apart from the way we came in, which I would have thought is only for emergencies."

"So how did the people here come and go, do you think?"

"That."

Esperance pointed towards a wide, flat area marked out with a giant H, now mostly faded. In the middle of the H was the hatch from which Esperance and Godriva had earlier emerged.

"Is that a helicopter landing zone?" Godriva asked.

"It is," Esperance confirmed. "We have one on the roof of the hospital."

The sound of grunting and yelling drifted their way. The blue savages beyond the fence had spotted them and were getting agitated, jumping up and down and waving their arms about. One of them even scaled the fence, but he didn't get far thanks to the razor wire.

"So freaky," said Godriva. "Do you think they are…like…ape men or something?"

"Can't be. Surely not."

There was a moment or two of silence, and then Godriva said, "I'm hungry. You said you found food."

"Are you sure you're up to eating anything? You've had a nasty shock, and your shoulder…"

"It must be the morphine. It's given me an appetite. And I have to keep eating so that Buki can keep feeding. Isn't that right, little man?"

Godriva bent forward and rubbed her nose against Buki's, causing him to giggle.

"Well, if you're sure," Esperance said. "I found the kitchens and the lights were on and the fridges and freezers were still working, so this building has power, thank god. Oh, and the toilets work. And the showers too. There's a canteen room as well. After we've eaten we can get cleaned up."

"I can't stop thinking about all the people on the boat who died," Godriva said. "Some of them were younger than us."

"I know. But we have to look after ourselves now. We have to survive."

Chapter 6

Hours later, after they had eaten and showered, the two sisters emerged from the sanctuary of the living block and stepped out into their new and enclosed world. The late afternoon sun was warm but not hot. However, humidity had now set in and the air was thick with flies. Esperance swatted them away with one arm as she marched purposefully across the helicopter landing zone. In the other arm she held Buki, and following closely behind was her sister. Their mission: to get a message out, to send for help.

As she trotted behind Esperance, Godriva tried her best to ignore the grunting and growling from the assembled blue savages beyond the fence. She failed.

"Oh god, I can't stand that noise they make," she complained through gritted teeth. She was still cradling her slinged-up arm. "I wish they'd stop!"

The communications room lay along one edge of the helicopter landing square. The door was ajar and so Esperance entered first. Dust swirled in the thin shards of light that cut in through the shutters. Godriva opened some of them fully, lighting the place up. What she was confronted with reminded her of the NASA control rooms she and her sister had seen on TV, with rows of computer consoles all facing a wall of large screens. But here there were no lights blinking, no computers humming and no screens flashing.

"Everything's dead," Esperance remarked. "Completely dead."

"Nice and cool in here, though, if nothing else," said Godriva.

"Cool isn't going to help us get out of here."

"Try the computers, then. See if you can get any of them going."

Buki seemed to be enjoying exploring with his mother and his aunt, and his large eyes sparkled with curiosity. Esperance tried hitting the monitor switches and moving the mice, but nothing happened. Godriva followed behind pulling out plugs and replacing them and hitting 'on' buttons, also with no result.

"There must be a master power switch somewhere," said Esperance. "Maybe built into the wall. See if any of these panels open."

The white walls, which seemed to be made of some form of fibreglass, were dotted with panels, some of which opened, many of which didn't. The ones that did revealed rows of switches and jacks for plugging things in, which was of no help.

"Oh, this is ridiculous!" Godriva grumbled. "There's got to be something we're missing."

"Let's try that other building."

Esperance and Godriva stepped back into the light and marched across the giant H. The blue men, who had started drifting away when the two tasty-looking morsels had disappeared, suddenly lunged back at the fence to continue their howling and their craving.

"If there's a master power switch somewhere, it's going to be in here," said Esperance upon entering the smaller building. It was sitting at a ninety-degree angle to the one they had just explored, along the helicopter landing square's other edge.

"What makes you think that?" Godriva asked as she followed her sister in.

"Ta-daa!"

There were no computer consoles to be found in this building, just miles of wiring, hundreds of jacks and plugs and about a dozen or so very large electrical switches.

"It's a nerd's wet dream," Esperance said with a smile.

She looked to her sister for a laugh or a smile in response, but there was nothing. Instead, Godriva continued to stare intensely at everything, as if searching for something particular.

"Actually," Esperance said, trying a different approach, "it looks like the racks room back at the hospital."

"What's a racks room?"

"It's where all the computer servers are, and where

all the telecommunications stuff is wired in, like the wi-fi and the phone lines."

"Wi-fi? Good. Let's try those," said Godriva, nodding towards the large electrical switches on the facing wall.

"You do it," Esperance said as she jiggled Buki up and down to keep him entertained.

The first switch was in the up position. Godriva grabbed hold of it with her left hand. It was stiff and took quite a lot of force to yank down. Nothing happened.

"Try pushing it back up," Esperance suggested.

Godriva pushed the switch back up to its original position, but still nothing happened.

"Oh, this is ridiculous!" Godriva moaned after trying the sixth switch. "We're wasting our time. And my arm hurts!"

As Godriva's irritability increased, so did her son's. He started crying.

"He might need changing," she said. "Let me see."

Esperance laid Buki down on one of the office chairs.

"Shush shush, my little man," Godriva cooed as she fussed over him. "We're not going to be here long. You'll see. We'll find a way off this island. We'll find a way."

"There's one more building to look at," Esperance said. "I think it might be a hangar."

They ventured back out into the humid daylight, blinking as they did so. Still, blue men were pacing up and down beyond the fence.

"You'd think they'd just get bored," Godriva grumbled.

Esperance led her sister over to a large concrete structure as Buki continued to sob and moan.

"Can you take him? I think he's had enough of me."

Esperance gently transferred the baby to Godriva's good arm.

"How long do I have to keep this sling on for? I want my arm back."

"Five days at least, I think."

The doors on the building, which accounted for almost its entire frontage, were on wheels and parted sideways easily and lightly.

"What's with the floor?" Godriva asked. A large section of the floor inside the hangar seemed to be movable. Also, there was a control console in the corner. "Is it a lift?"

"It must be," said Esperance. "I think there's a great deal more to this place underground."

"But there's no power so we can't get down there."

"Except for down that hatch in the airlock. But that door didn't open so there has to be another way. Has to be. God, this is so frustrating! I can't help feeling that all the really interesting stuff is right below our feet!"

Fed up, they made their way back to the living block rooftop, grabbing a couple of bottles of chilled water from the kitchen on the way. Esperance plonked herself down onto a lounger, hands wringing, foot tapping.

"Tomorrow we can go through all the other bunk rooms," she said with an air of determination. "See what we can salvage. Maybe we can find a clue as to how to get the power back on."

Godriva was peering over the edge of the roof garden. "There's still a few of those blue men down there, look. They haven't gone away."

"That's because they want to kill us."

Buki was feeling left out and forgotten about, so he reminded his mother and his aunt of his presence by murmuring.

"He's hungry," said Godriva. She lifted her vest and put her baby to her breast.

Seeing the look of yearning in Buki's eyes helped to ease the knot of frustration that had been forming in Esperance's stomach, so she allowed herself to relax a little. If the three of them were in this for the long haul, then so be it. At least they had somewhere comfortable to sleep and an almost endless supply of food. Also, they were safe from the horrors that still lurked outside.

"You feed Buki and I'll feed us," she said. "It's dinner time."

Around twenty minutes later, she returned carrying a tray.

"I found macaroni cheese in the freezer so I microwaved it. And I got some biscuits too. And I made coffee. We'll not go hungry tonight."

They sat and ate without speaking, both too tired, neither knowing what to say. And then, as the horizon swallowed the sun, something happened.

"Esperance. Look at the sky," Godriva said between mouthfuls. "Have you ever seen anything like it?"

"No," Esperance replied. "I haven't. Ever."

Above their new island home, the darkening sky had come alive with stars, vivid, intense and shimmering. And that was not all. An incandescent band had appeared, arcing with swirling colours across the heavens.

"Is that the Milky Way?" an enchanted Esperance asked.

"It must be," Godriva gasped.

"It looks so close, like we could reach out and touch it. It's incredible."

The sisters continued to sit and stare in silence for a while, absentmindedly spooning macaroni cheese into their mouths. Eventually, Godriva broke the silence.

"I can't figure out the door," she said. "The one in the tunnel. What were the odds of me hitting the right numbers to open it?"

"Somebody up there was obviously looking out for us."

"I hope you're not about to suggest that god opened the door for us."

Esperance smiled. "No. But someone."

On this point, she was partially right. Someone had been looking out for them, but they weren't in the heavens above, she was on the other side of the world and her name was Cynthia.

When the sky reached a deep cosmic-blue and the night air became cold, the two sisters and the baby returned to the safety of their bunkroom to try and sleep. Meanwhile, in the sky above, amid the shimmering stars, things began to move.

***

No more giant blue savages came that day. Vital, still hiding out on the upper level of the dilapidated warehouse and still on high alert, had no idea how many hours he'd been watching and listening. He'd had no food or water since the night before and his throat and stomach were burning. Also, he had started to feel weak and sleepy. He didn't want to succumb to sleep, however. He was afraid to.

As well as all the junk and the cubicles on the upper level, there was a view. A large, rectangular section of the wall was missing, presenting Vital with a vista. He supposed that before the storm there had been a door of some sort over it, which could be opened to allow fork-lift trucks to deposit goods straight onto the upper floor. From here he could see the plain, the rocky outcrop and the jungle by the beach where the lifeboat had come ashore. It all seemed like so long ago, even though barely more than twelve hours had passed. But the sun was setting now, sending long blue shadows snaking across the pink ground, and the birds were growing quiet.

Vital sat cross legged on the floor, facing the scene, and fished his phone out of his back pocket. He had long since given up checking for signal. There was none to be had here. He opened the contacts and scrolled through until he came to Walter. He couldn't imagine ever deleting his best friend's name and number. He knew that Walter would only cease to exist completely once the trail of electronic data he'd left behind had dissolved. Strange, really.

He swiped through to his text messages and opened the last one received from his fallen friend. It said: *Where ru???* Vital had been running late on the day they had fled Burundi. Not much of an epitaph. He opened his photos and scrolled down, looking for one in particular. It was a selfie, obviously, featuring Vital and Walter smiling widely and throwing the obligatory V-signs. Vital had taken it inside the Prince Louis Rwagasore Stadium in Burundi about three months previously. In the background, on the pitch, were two football teams, neither of which was Manchester United.

Vital's mind drifted back to 2012 when Man U had toured South Africa. How excited he and Walter had been, knowing that their beloved team were so close. They hadn't been close, of course – nowhere near close – but to their young minds the team might as well have been just a few streets away. They had pored over game footage and match reports and entertained flights of fancy in which this fabled team then came to nearby

Kenya, neighbouring Tanzania or even Burundi itself.

Walter's dream of playing for them had died with him, needless to say, and for Vital himself it now seemed irretrievably beyond reach. Never mind playing for Man U, it would be a miracle if he even managed to get off this island! He detached himself from his grim reverie and looked out over his new kingdom. The sky had turned from red to purple now and was alive with stars, shining intensely.

They're never that bright back at home, he mused.

Low over the distant jungle a silver pill-shaped craft was hovering. Vital sprang up from his sitting position and stared dumbly at this thing that should not be. This island, it seemed, was full of things that should not be, and while Vital had been daydreaming about football, the universe had come calling.

He knew all about UFOs and aliens. He and Walter had once upon a time enjoyed scaring each other shitless with online videos that boasted GENUINE ALIEN FOOTAGE or REAL ALIENS CAUGHT ON TAPE and TERRIFYING UFO FILM WILL LEAVE YOU SPEECHLESS! They would always make the mistake of watching these things just before retiring to their respective beds for the night, where the shaky, night-vision images would grow and fester, eventually mutating into nightmares.

The craft moved suddenly and Vital jumped. He hid behind a steel pillar and peeked out. Then the craft lurched horizontally, too fast to be permitted by basic

61

physics, and then vertically. It streaked upwards and stopped suddenly, as if someone had pressed the pause button on a DVD. It left behind it a trail, but not one of smoke or vapour. It was more like a distortion, as if the sky was reordering itself in its wake. Then the mysterious craft vanished, streaking away into nothingness.

When's this going to end? Vital thought.

***

As the boy from Burundi was starting to wonder about his sleeping arrangements for the night, on the other side of the world a plane was kissing tarmac and pulling to a stop.

Tyler, aka Captain Buck Rogers, opened the door and lowered the steps, allowing the weary passengers to spill out into the cold morning. Among them was Cynthia who was eager to get home, crash into bed and forget all about what must qualify as the strangest night shift she'd ever pulled. But first there was the matter of breakfast, and the sweet aromas from Gene's Hot Dog Heaven trailer were calling to her.

Gene was not on flipping and frying duty this morning. Instead, it was his son Antonio behind the skillet. Antonio was huge and all but filled the trailer. On his head he wore his obligatory Cardinals cap, backwards, of course.

"Hey, Antonio," Cynthia muttered. "Where's the old

man?"

"Having a well-earned lie in, so here I am. You ain't your usual cheery self this morning. Whassup?"

"Just work stuff. Nothing heavy. Been a long night."

Oh, but it was heavy. Ed had taken Cynthia aside and torn a strip off her for letting civilians into the lab site.

"What was I supposed to do?" Cynthia had not unreasonably asked. "Sit there and watch as those blue guys ripped them apart?"

"You don't know that's what they'd have done," Ed had replied, making not a great deal of sense.

"Um. Yes I do. They were out of their minds, feral, like wild animals. And besides, one of those women had a baby."

"Well, I never thought you of all people would go all mushy over a baby."

Cynthia had squared up to him at this. "I hope you're not suggesting that just because I'm a lesbian I don't like babies."

Ed had seen an official complaint followed by a compulsory Respect and Diversity Training Module flash before his eyes.

"No, of course not," he'd gulped. "But you can expect there to be serious consequences for your actions today. Mark my words."

Words marked, Cynthia had returned to her workstation.

"That's okay then," Antonio said. "Now, what can I getcha?"

Cynthia devoured her fantastically unhealthy yet sensationally tasty breakfast in welcome silence on the bus home.

The short plane hop, on the other hand, had been a far livelier affair, and had seen her fielding a multitude of questions about the two women and the baby – "Don't know any more than you." – about the blue men – "How the fuck am I supposed to know?" – and about her roasting from Ed – "Ed's a creep. He likes to think he's some big company hotshot, but Mr B doesn't even know he exists."

Chapter 7

Apparently it was Cynthia Dowley who let the two young women into the compound. Obviously, she acted with the best of intentions – they did have a baby with them, after all – but she really opened a can of worms when she did that. For a start, there's the security issue. Those two young women have now stumbled right into the middle of one of the most significant and, yes, dangerous scientific experiments in history. If they get any of the comms going they could blow everything, and the last thing this shitshow needs right now is another disaster. One's enough for any man! And what's more it's only a matter of time before Victor realises they're there, if he hasn't already, and then god knows what'll happen. I mean, what if he gets them to restart The Machine? I wouldn't put it past him, despite what happened the last time. Anyway, all this has now been fed up to Mr B so I think we can expect a visit sooner rather than later.

But it's Cynthia I feel most sorry for. I don't know what she's like outside of work but when she's here she's straight down the line, dependable, never complains or causes trouble. But when she hit the button to open that emergency door, like it or not she went and dumped a whole ton of horse manure on herself. Shame, really.

Journal entry dated 8th Jan 2018

***

Some fourteen or so hours after morning had arrived in Arizona, it finally illuminated this mysterious island off the East Africa coast. Here in the bunkroom, where no light penetrated, it was impossible to know where the sun was in the sky, or even if it was in the sky at all.

At various times during the night, Esperance, who had sunk deeper into sleep than the *Dream Angus* had into the ocean, had become vaguely aware of noise and movement; Godriva, up with Buki who needed changing, feeding, reassuring or all three. And each time, Esperance, having assured herself that she was not in fact still on the stricken vessel, allowed herself to be pulled back under the drowsy waves and swept along on the tide of her dreams.

For her sister, on the other hand, sleep was now a stranger. She no longer detached herself completely from the world to become fully immersed in the rejuvenating thrall of slumber. Instead, a section of her mind remained on sentry duty, ever monitoring the rhythm of Buki's breathing, the tempo of his heartbeat, the frequency of his tiny murmurings. All it took now was a single sob to drag Godriva back from the black abyss, and within no more than three heartbeats she would be holding him, rocking him, shushing him.

Esperance stirred, blearily fumbled for her phone and pressed the button on the side. The screen came alive and told her that the time was 5:15a.m. It also told her, rather alarmingly, that she only had 6% battery power left. Clad only in a pair of knickers and a light vest, both in desperate need of a wash, she got out of bed and staggered into the *en suite* bathroom to use the toilet.

Godriva opened her eyes and felt for the switch next to her bunk, then scrunched them up as they were assaulted by the light. Buki was already awake and murmuring softly to himself. Godriva had utilised a drawer as a cot, placing him on a big fluffy towel and wrapping him loosely in a smaller hand towel. There was no sign of Esperance, but then Godriva heard the toilet flush from beyond the bathroom door and relaxed somewhat. Her little family unit was still all present and correct.

"You're awake," Esperance said with a yawn as she stepped back into the room. "How's your arm?"

"Stiff and sore," Godriva grumbled. "It kept me up most of the night, along with Buki. Where are you going?"

"To find something to wear," said Esperance as she exited the room. "I can't put on the same clothes again today. They're disgusting."

Esperance and Godriva had chosen this particular bunkroom because it appeared unused. Actually, it was one of several unused bunkrooms. The previous evening, the sisters had helped themselves to a quick peek into the other ones and had seen lots of personal belongings lying around; books, clothes, photos, phones. But the previous evening they had been in no mood to go prying into the private lives of the mysteriously missing, and so they had left everything untouched. Today, however, was a different story, so when Esperance returned to their cosy sanctuary, she was wearing a blue boiler suit, tied off at the waist.

"Found it a few doors along," she explained. "There's another one there if you want it."

"No, thank you. Is there a laundry, do you know?" Godriva asked. "I need to wash Buki's things."

"Yes. In the basement. One of the women must have been an engineer," Esperance said, returning to the subject of her new attire. "Obviously about our size, too. We'll have to go through everyone's stuff and see what we can salvage."

"Seems a bit…I don't know…wrong somehow."

"I know, but this is survival now. We have no choice. Besides, I need to charge my phone. There must be a few chargers lying around."

"Probably find one in every room," said Godriva.

Esperance went over to Buki, snug in his makeshift cot, and started unwrapping him.

He looked up at his aunt, somehow understanding that the face gazing down on him was not his mother's despite it appearing almost identical. Nevertheless, that face radiated love and safety, and so he smiled.

"It's breakfast time for the little man," Godriva said. "Pass him to me."

Esperance did so and turned to leave the room once again.

"Where are you going now?"

"To raid the kitchen."

"How are we for milk?"

"Okay. There's still some unopened in the fridges, and there's long-life and powdered in the storeroom."

"If there's cereal, can you fetch me some?"

"There's cereal."

With Esperance gone, Godriva, with baby now at her breast, picked up her phone and started scrolling through the photos, much as Vital had done the night before in his considerably less comfortable surroundings. She found a pic of herself with Benjamin and immediately felt tears forming.

When Benjamin had died he had been stripped of the opportunity to ever become slovenly, selfish or inattentive, and so he was fixed in Godriva's mind and heart as someone pure, blameless and completely beyond reproach. He had become an angel.

Godriva scrolled past the picture and came to a photo of herself, Esperance and their brother Aloÿs, which had been taken a few years back on a long white beach.

Aloÿs was now a health worker in Muyinga, Burundi's second city. When he had found out about his sisters' intention to leave the country, he had implored them not to go.

"Terrible things happen to unaccompanied women," he had cried down the phone. "Terrible things! The world doesn't care about refugees!"

Turns out he was right, thought Godriva.

***

Vital did not awaken gently or easily, greeting the new day with a luxurious stretch and a comfortable yawn. Instead, he sprang up, startled, into a fight-or-flight stance with his eyes bulging and his fists clenched.

In his sleep he had heard the dying cries of his friend Walter and had seen a wild blue giant with a mouthful of blood charging. And now here he was, mind and heart racing, brain and body on full alert. But Walter was no more and the blue savage was also dead. Or at least, Vital hoped so.

Before darkness had completely overcome the old warehouse that was now his sanctuary, he had carried out a quick recce and had struck something approximating gold. The small cubicles/offices each contained if not a desk, then at the very least the remains of one. Vital had gone through all the drawers and had found, in amongst the staplers, post-it notes, diaries, pens and printer cartridges, two bottles of water, a can

70

of coke, a box of cereal bars (out of date, but who cares?) and a packet of chewing gum. He had also found a sofa. Yes, a sofa. It was not in the best condition, but it was dry and it meant Vital was spared having to sleep on the floor. What luxury!

But, unsurprisingly, he had not slept easily. Every time he had started to drift off some noise had startled him awake again. This had gone on pretty much all night, and in his fleeting moments of sleep he had been tormented by thoughts of Walter. One image kept returning, repeating over and over like a broken DVD; that of his friend standing under the morning sun on the dusty plain, completely motionless and wearing a look of cool serenity on his face as a pack of blue savages charged at him from behind with murderous intent.

This reminded Vital of the dead blue man under the motorbike. With his legs still aching from the previous day's sprinting, he walked stiffly over to the big square hole in the floor. The dead blue man was still dead and lying underneath the motorbike with flies buzzing all around him. Vital breathed out. The mysterious flying object he had seen in the sky the night before wasn't causing him any more worry either. Its potential threat had been relegated to a lower division by the reassuring beams of morning sunlight. And besides, unlike the unfortunate blue man below, the silver craft had not tried to kill him.

He was fully awake now and his mind was galloping with thoughts and plans and possibilities, all pertaining to getting the hell off this crazy island. Oh, but Walter. Walter would not be by his side, and never would be again. What to do? Vital was torn between sticking with the plan, in honour of his friend, and trying to continue on to the UK, or giving up and going home. After all, Walter's parents deserved to know what had happened to their boy, even though they would never believe it.

Vital could feel a headache coming on. There was too much to consider and a mountain of thinking to do. But besides, he was feeling the call of nature now, and so he went off to find somewhere to urinate.

As he pissed out of the side of the building and onto the dusty ground below, he decided on a plan for the day. It felt good to have a course of action mapped out. It gave him something to focus on. He was going to walk to the big hill that dominated the island, climb it, and from the summit see if he could spot any obvious shipping lanes out at sea. The lifeboat was still hidden in the trees by the beach somewhere, so if he could see a shipping lane he could heave the boat back into the water, row in that general direction and hope for the best. Of course, this plan involved him running the risk of bumping into those blue savages again, but he couldn't see any other way of escape. His mind was made up.

***

Esperance and Godriva, with her right arm still in its

sling and her baby cradled in the other, stepped out into the cool morning sunshine and wandered across the helicopter landing zone. A fresh breeze wafted over the compound, bringing with it the revitalising scent of the ocean.

Esperance had not given up on finding a way to send out a message for help. "Even if it's just a message in a bottle," she had said.

Godriva had been unconvinced. "But if all the computers are dead and there's no signal or Wi-Fi. How can we…?"

But Esperance had cut her off. "Look, if we're going to get off this insane island we have to work together. It's not enough for you to just moan and grumble while I do all the work. You have to help me. Neither of us are stupid. You're a schoolteacher for goodness' sake. We'll find a way."

Esperance stopped dead in the middle of the H. No blue savages had gathered at the fence as yet so all was quiet, which was welcome. She pointed at the huge satellite dish on top of the comms building they had explored the previous day.

"Look at that. What can that be for if not sending signals? There has to be a way to get it working. We must be missing something."

But on this she was wrong. The dish was most certainly not for sending signals.

"We are not engineers," Godriva mumbled. "What can we possibly do?" Esperance fixed her with a look

73

and Godriva checked herself. "Okay. Okay. We'll figure it out. At least we're safe in here while we do."

"Exactly! And we're not going to starve and…and…"

"What is it, sister? What's the matter?"

Something had transfixed Esperance. She was walking slowly towards the outer fence as if in a trance.

"Esperance? What's…oh god."

Beyond the thankfully impenetrable fence, a cloud of dust was fast approaching across the plain. Godriva started to back away.

"Let's get inside," she breathed. "Sister? Come. Let's get inside."

The cloud was close enough now for vague human shapes to be discerned. Blue human shapes.

"You go," said Esperance, who was still staring out across the wide expanse. "Take Buki."

"You must come too. It's not safe out here."

But Esperance was unnervingly calm. "They can't get through the fence. It's okay. You go."

The savages were coming *en masse*, sprinting, charging, yelling. Esperance got to within four feet of the fence before stopping. Then she waited.

"Sister!" Godriva called one last time from the living block door.

Esperance turned and gestured for her sister to go. Reluctantly, Godriva entered the building, shut the door behind her and fled to the safety of the bunkroom with her baby.

The blue men were almost at the fence now. Esperance counted eight of them, a hive-mind of rage, ferocity and frenzy. Every pair of murderous yellow eyes was focused on the young woman, their prey. The rampaging blue bodies collided with the fence as one, but even with such force and power they barely rattled it. Some started climbing, some shook the cables and some reached through to try and grab her.

Esperance was not fazed. She started slowly walking back and fore along the line of blue bodies that was now on such animated display before her, studying them, analysing them. They really were all incredibly tall, around seven feet. Also, they were all tightly muscled, with no body fat whatsoever, and completely devoid of body hair. Their yellow eyes reminded Esperance of those of big cats. And then she noticed something truly astonishing, something to do with their features. It was clear that some of these blue men had once been Caucasian, some of them Asian and some of them Black, like Esperance herself. But now they were all blue-skinned and yellow-eyed and running in a pack like wild animals.

A dark thought crossed Esperance's mind.

Chapter 8

"Say, those two part o' yer gang?"

Gene nodded towards a pair of too-clean-cut-to-be-true loiterers. They were a man and a woman, both in their mid-to-late thirties. The male, dark haired, was casually dressed in jeans and black jacket with a paperback in hand. The female, a redhead, was stylishly attired and was staring at her phone. They were both wearing sunglasses and sitting on suitcases.

"Never seen 'em before," Cynthia said. "Don't know 'bout anyone new starting either."

The old hot dog maestro flagged them as government people. It was the clothes that gave them away, apparently. They looked so darn new, like straight-off-the-peg new. Cynthia watched through narrowed eyes as they both wandered over to the runway where the spaceport plane was taxiing to a halt.

"Came in earlier in a Hummer. That's it over there."

"A Hummer? Jeez! Not short of a few bucks then."

"Nope. Now then, you hungry or aintcha?"

Cynthia had a bad feeling about these two strangers,

but not bad enough to cause any slowdown in her appetite, so she had a coffee (large), a dog (with cheese, ketchup and mustard) and a pretzel.

Later, in the monitoring room, she leant over to Matt at the next workstation. "Hey, did you see those new guys on the plane earlier? Sat at the back? He was reading a book?"

"What book was it?" Matt asked.

"I don't know what fucking book it was," an incredulous Cynthia hissed. "I wasn't looking *that* closely. Jesus, Matt, you need to get your priorities straight."

"How do you mean?"

"Shit goes down at work. Some guy from Central Security tells us the company's being experimenting on people. Next day some new guys are on the plane. Isn't it obvious these things are connected?"

Matt looked unconvinced. "But they could be just that, a couple of new guys."

"They always tell us when there's fresh meat for the grinder. Besides, I didn't like the way he looked at me on the plane."

"Who? This new guy?"

"Yeah."

"Oh, you're just being paranoid," Matt said. "Well, don't worry, kiddo. Experience has taught me that the machinations of the rich and shameless inevitably turn out to be far more mundane than we first suspect. Nothing's gonna happen to you. You'll see."

"Cynthia. Can you come with me, please?" It was Ed.

Cynthia turned to Matt. "You were saying?"

Ed was a company man through and through. His sole purpose for existing was to serve his billionaire overlord, Byron Wurd. When not fawning over his superiors at the spaceport he would sit in front of his PC at home, single-handedly patrolling the internet, looking for blogs and posts that had anything negative to say about his glorious employer. He would then seethe and boil with rage, 'setting them straight' and 'correcting' them. Educating them as to what a fine and benevolent man the company's founder was.

Needless to say, he was despised by the people who worked under him, including Cynthia. As she followed him past her staring colleagues and into the conference room, she pictured him in a 1920s bellboy uniform, laden with luggage, cravenly following Mr B through a grand hotel lobby and simpering, "Yes, sir. No, sir. Lick your shoes clean, sir? Why, that would be my pleasure, sir."

In the conference room, Cynthia found two people waiting for her.

"You've got to be shitting me," she said. Out loud.

The people waiting for her did not react. No, they were far too cool for that, because they were Men in Black. Or rather, one man and one woman in black.

"This is Al Leon and Champagne Star," Ed said as he wrung his hands and shifted from foot to foot. "They're with the CIA and they want to talk to you about…"

Ed's words congealed into background sludge as Cynthia's jaw fell open. "The CIA?"

"Don't worry," said the man in black. "You're not in any trouble."

"I'm not?"

"She's not?" Ed echoed, clearly disappointed.

This Al Leon guy ignored him. Then the lady in black spoke: "You *are* Cynthia Dowley, aren't you?" she asked from behind her shades.

Cynthia peered at her closely. Then at him. Then back at her.

"Hang on," she said. "You're the guys I saw on the plane earlier. You were reading a book, you were looking at your cell. I knew you were watching me. Presumably your Men in Black costumes were in your suitcases, then."

For just a second, the visitors looked unsure of what to do. This snarky young lady was not sticking to the script.

"Cynthia Dowley?" the woman in black asked again.

Cynthia rolled her eyes. "Look, if you're gonna fire me, I'd rather you just got on with it than keep me in suspense, know what I mean?"

Ed threw his hands in the air in a gesture of exasperation. "Will you *please* just confirm your name?"

"Okay okay! Yes, I'm Cynthia Dowley."

"Thank you," said Al, aka the Man in Black. "Our

visit is in regard to the incident that occurred yesterday at SpaceWurd's East Africa laboratory, into which you admitted three civilians; two females and an infant of indeterminate sex."

Cynthia looked unsure. "Okaaaaaay."

Champagne, aka the Woman in Black, carried on, "Two days ago, as you know, there was a major security breach at the lab facility, resulting in the deaths of the research staff. As Neal Terry explained to you yesterday, they died at the hands of the test subjects. While you were in the boardroom being debriefed, the emergency door that you monitor was opened by one of the Central Security team and the test subjects were allowed to escape the facility."

"They have since found shelter in an area of jungle that stretches along the coastline," Al added.

Champagne continued, "The two women you admitted through that same emergency door are refugees. They, and the baby, were among a party of eight that washed up on the beach. They were then set upon by the test subjects. The two women managed to get away and make it to the facility."

"Where I let them in."

"Where you let them in."

"Yeah, about that…" said Cynthia, ready to launch into her defence, but she was cut off.

"No one's going to penalise you for saving the lives of two women and a baby," said Al, "We all would have done the same."

Cynthia shot Ed a look. He looked down at his shoes.

"Well, great," said Cynthia. "So now you can go and rescue those refugees and…"

"I'm afraid it's not that simple," Champagne said, talking over Cynthia.

"I had a feeling you were going to say that. So where does the CIA fit into all this?"

"There was a classified project in progress at the facility," Champagne explained. "A machine was in development that was destabilised during the incident, and it could blow at any moment."

"And if it does," said Al, "it'll take that entire island with it."

"Oh," was all Cynthia could manage.

Champagne continued, "We're here to help your Central Security department stabilise this machine, clean up the mess and hopefully get the project back on track."

"And rescue the two women and the kid," Cynthia added.

"Yeah. That too."

Cynthia was unconvinced. It started to dawn on her that perhaps the rescue of these refugees was not terribly high on the priority list of these mysterious visitors. Al, in turn, realised that they were not going to get this Cynthia girl on board without an assurance that the refugees would be saved.

"Look," he began. "The two ladies and the child are still in danger, even inside the facility, but in order to help them we need you to help us. With that in mind, we've been authorised to offer you a promotion to the Central Security team."

"What?" gasped Cynthia.

"What?" gasped Ed.

Cynthia quickly regained her composure. "Does it come with a raise?"

"No it does not come with a raise!" snapped Ed, whose face had turned bright red.

"Yes, it comes with a raise," Al confirmed.

"Then yes. I accept." Cynthia directed this acceptance, which came complete with a very wide smile, at Ed.

"Good," said Al. "I'll pass the good news on to our superiors and to Central Security and they'll give you the details. In the meantime, just carry on as normal."

"So, what book were you reading?" Cynthia asked, going off topic.

"Pardon?"

"What book were you reading? At the airport and on the plane?"

Cynthia noticed a look of uncertainty shared between the visitors, then Al lowered his shades and fixed her with a stare as if he were trying to hypnotise her. "I was not at the airport this morning," he said," and neither was my colleague. We did not board any plane."

"Okaaaay," said a wide-eyed Cynthia as she backed away. "I'll just go back to my station now, if it's all the same to you guys."

"What was that?" Ed feebly enquired after she'd gone. "If anyone should be promoted to the top tier, it's me! I've been here longer than anyone in this department, and what's more I've always served this company loyally, shown nothing but the utmost respect to Mr Wurd. And…"

Throughout this rant, Al and Champagne continued to stare blankly at him.

"…she doesn't even make an effort to dress professionally! Have you seen all the tattoos she's got? And that hairstyle? And the piercings! Oh sure, it may be what all the kids are doing nowadays, but in my day…"

Finally, Champagne stepped forward and flatly stated: "Believe me, this isn't a step up for her. Quite the opposite. You're far better off staying where you are now."

And with that the visitors left.

Chapter 9

Vital had yet to see any wild blue giants so far today, but he was still running for his life. Approaching the hill, where the dusty terrain gave way to rocks and desiccated trees, the ground had come suddenly alive. Snakes oozed from the cracks in the rocks and snapped at his ankles. They were small and fast with yellow eyes and a skin pattern of dark brown and tan. Luckily, Vital was protected by his trainers and his jeans, but he still felt a sharp nip with every strike. He skipped out of the way and backed off, jumping as he felt more nips on his calves. He wheeled around to see the ground literally writhing. There were thousands of them, springing up from the dust like little coils, biting and nipping at his legs. He ran for the hill. Bad idea.

It was in amongst the rocks where it was relatively cool that the snakes lived, and Vital was sprinting deeper into their domain. Every bite was like a tiny electrical shock. He could die right here, right now, he knew. This grim realisation took him beyond fear, and cold panic took over. Vital screamed and kicked and ran for a nearby tree, an ash-white skeleton of trunk and branches that had long since forgotten the colour of green. He jumped for a high branch but it snapped off in his hand, sending him crashing back down. He knew that if he lost his balance and fell, this living carpet would take only a few seconds to completely smother him and then it would be game over. He quickly regained his footing, threw his arms around a low, thick tree branch and clambered up.

Snakes were whipping up the trunk now, still snapping at him. He did not want to die like this, as the result of a million little bites. He could think of no worse way to go. Shaking and sweating, Vital scrambled up and up until he could go no further. He was too high for the snakes now, but he was trapped. Below him, the ground continued to squirm.

**

The bunkrooms were all identical, save for the personal belongings. With Buki sleeping soundly in his drawer-cot, Esperance and Godriva quietly and respectfully explored each one in turn, looking for things they could use.

The first room they tried belonged to a male who was evidently quite large, judging by the clothes hanging in the closet, folded up in the drawers and strewn about the floor. There was a laptop on the desk, but without the password it was useless. Plugged into the laptop was a

PlayStation, and next to the PlayStation a tablet computer. Again, useless without the PIN code. Next to the tablet was an MP3 player.

"So much stuff," said Godriva. "And none of it any good to us."

She sifted through the desk drawers; wallet, set of keys, pens, notepad.

Something caught Esperance's eye on the shelf above one of the bunks. Technical manuals, piled high, each one featuring a well-known logo on the front. She picked one off at random and opened it.

"What is it?" Godriva asked.

"It's a manual," Esperance replied. "It says SpaceWurd on it."

"SpaceWurd. Aren't they supposed to be sending passengers into space? Is it all science stuff?"

"Yes. Way beyond me."

"I can't believe SpaceWurd own this site and they haven't sent anyone to help. They must know we're here."

"Perhaps. Perhaps not. But something very bad happened here. It's obvious."

Esperance replaced the manual and tried another one. Again, it was very technical, very specialised. She made a mental note to come back later and gather them all up with the intention of going through them. A suspicion had formed in her mind, and she was hopeful these manuals would either confirm or refute it once and for all. Preferably refute.

As she was putting the manual back she noticed a framed photograph. It featured a man, a woman and a child. The man was large, bearded, smiling. His hair was dark but shaved off at the sides and he had a large 'gauge' in the lobe of each ear. The woman in the picture looked tiny next to him. She had long, blacker-than-night hair, heavy eye make-up and a piercing in her lower lip. The child was a girl aged around four, by Esperance's reckoning. She was blonde, smiling and wearing a pink dress, which provided a welcome splash of colour against the black clothing of her parents.

"Where's your daddy gone, little girl?" Esperance whispered.

"What was that?"

"Nothing. Anything interesting in there?"

Godriva was poking around in the tiny *en suite* bathroom. Every bunk room had one, with a toilet, sink, mirror and small shower.

"Toothpaste, toothbrush, shower gel. Just what you'd expect. Oh, and haemorrhoid cream."

"Lovely."

The next bunkroom proved far more useful.

"This is where I got this from," said Esperance, tugging at the arm of the blue boiler suit she was wearing.

Godriva went straight for the wardrobe as Esperance made for the bathroom.

"There's lots of stuff here we can salvage," Godriva said, pulling out a pair of olive-green khaki shorts.

"Oh, thank goodness!" Esperance cried from the little *en suite*. "There's shampoo, conditioner, moisturisers, nice shower gels, not like the man had. There's even a brand-new toothbrush, unopened."

Godriva held the khaki shorts up against herself. "Whoever lives here has excellent taste in clothes," she said.

Esperance was pleased to hear her sister talking about the occupant of this room in the present tense. It meant that Godriva believed she might still be alive somewhere, which in turn meant she was still holding out hope. Esperance then turned her attention to the desk.

"Let's see…laptop, tablet, same as last time. Diary. I'm not going to look through that. Purse. Phone. Looks like it's died already. Lots of candy in here too."

"Candy? Let me see."

Godriva nudged her sister out of the way and went rummaging through the drawer.

"M&Ms, Reeses, popcorn, Snickers. Thank you, god!"

Esperance was grateful for this small mercy which might go some way to alleviate her sister's black mood.

As Godriva tore open a bag of M&Ms, Esperance checked out the manuals on the shelf above the bunk. Again, they were incredibly advanced, showing machine diagrams, computer coding, chemical formulas, all of which was alien to her. In this room also was a framed photo by the bunk, this one was of a beautiful tortoiseshell cat.

"Cute kitty," Esperance whispered.

The next room was another male one, judging by the number of used tissues in the bin under the desk. There wasn't much of interest for Esperance and Godriva here, just man-sized clothing, the usual laptop and tablet and yet more manuals, until…

"Oh. My. God."

"What is it?" Esperance asked with genuine concern. "What's the matter?"

Godriva pulled a small device from a desk drawer.

"It's only a Nintendo Switch! Look!" Godriva held it up for Esperance to see, but she only sighed.

"Godriva! You frightened me! I thought something was wrong."

"No. Not wrong. Definitely right. I wonder what games there are."

And for the first time since washing ashore on this accursed island, Godriva smiled. Esperance felt her entire body relax a little at this.

"Come here," she said.

She wrapped her arms around her confused sister's shoulders and pulled her in close for a hug.

"We'll get through this," Esperance said. "We just have to be strong, and help each other."

A tear or two fell from Esperance's eyes and trickled down Godriva's back. Godriva felt them and returned Esperance's hug. And then the Earth came alive.

"What the…?" Esperance gasped, pulling away from

Godriva. "Do you feel that?"

Two or three of the technical manuals fell from the shelf onto the bed.

"Is it an earthquake?" Godriva asked, her eyes wide with fear.

"Perhaps we should get Buki and go outside."

"Yes. I'll go fetch him…"

And then the tremor stopped. Esperance and Godriva stood in silence for a moment, listening and waiting.

"Is it over?" Godriva pondered.

"Seems like it. When was the last time we had an earthquake? I mean back home?"

"Burundi isn't my home anymore."

Esperance could sense Godriva's black mood returning. She needed to have her sister onside, not constantly teetering at the edge of a pit of despair.

"I'll check the bathroom," she said. And then with a cheeky wink added, "You look around to see what games there are for your Nintendo."

The smile returned to Godriva's face.

As Esperance made a mental inventory of the contents of the bathroom, she listened to Godriva making an inventory of her own: "Mario, Zelda, Pokémon. This is amazing! Where's the charger?"

Esperance enjoyed a little smile at the sound of Godriva regressing just a little to the happy girl she had once been.

If a few computer games are what it takes to help you get through this, Esperance thought, *then so be it*.

That Godriva had been the one to propose fleeing Burundi to make a new life in another country had been a surprise to everyone, except Esperance. Godriva had always been the one to resist change and Esperance the more adventurous of the two. Their mother Ines had seen this reflected in their career choices. As a nurse, Esperance had to act reactively, as there was no telling what manner of emergency would be next to come crashing out of the back of an ambulance. It was a vocation in which no two days were ever the same. But in complete contrast, as a schoolteacher, Godriva's days were timetabled. She always knew exactly what the day would have in store for her, so she could be prepared. And that was just how she liked it.

But Esperance had seen the resolve of her sister crumble to dust as she had nursed the dying Benjamin. Godriva, by this time heavily pregnant, had barely left her boyfriend's bedside during those four long, terrible days. And with the passing of every day, as Benjamin moved ever closer to his death, Godriva's light grew just a little bit dimmer.

"Benji said if we had a son he wanted to call him Bukeneza," Godriva had said as she cradled her baby in her arms for the first time. "So that's what I'm going to name him. Bukeneza. But I am not going to raise him here. People are always fighting in Burundi. He will not be safe."

"But where will you go?" Ines had asked, her eyes filling up with tears. "You have family here. Support.

Me. Your sister."

"We have already decided. We are going to South Africa."

"But why South Africa?"

"Because it's not Burundi, that's why."

***

After roughly an hour and forty minutes spent clinging uncomfortably to the precarious apex of the dried-out tree, Vital was feeling hot, hungry and weak. Below him, the ground continued to squirm and writhe. Every snake on the island, it seemed, had come out to see him. Thousands of pairs of tiny, evil eyes regarded him hungrily.

Vital wanted to scream at them to go away, to leave him alone, but something he had spotted in the distance had convinced him that screaming may not be such a good idea. From his vantage point he could see right across the plain, the plain that was now shimmering in the humid afternoon, and scattered about the vast expanse of dirt and grass, grazing like sheep, were a number of those blue savages. The last thing Vital wanted to do was alert them to his presence by yelling at snakes.

Just as desperation was starting to take hold of him, a miracle happened. In the scheme of things it was not a great miracle – it was actually quite a minor one – but to Vital it was a very big deal indeed.

It started to rain.

It was one of those intense, torrential downpours that only happens in tropical climes and starts and departs in mere minutes. Dark, bulbous clouds materialised from nowhere, turning the sky black. Thunder boomed across the island and Vital saw the blue dots on the plain all running for the jungle. The savages were frightened, frightened of the terrific noise they could not understand.

The raindrops that followed were heavy and each and every one hit the ground with a splash, sending the snakes wriggling away to hide in the cracks and crevices of the rocks. In less than a minute there was not a snake to be seen. Vital, now sopping wet and grateful for it, clambered quickly down from his sanctuary and sprinted up the hill. Then a thought occurred to him.

If it stops raining while I'm up there, how am I going to get back down without meeting all those snakes again?

Chapter 10

Well, I suppose it was inevitable. The place is crawling with government men, and experience tells me when that happens things tend to get messy. And now the spooks are here you can bet Mr B ain't gonna be far behind with that darn entourage of his. Great. But anyway, in the meantime there's been another powwow and it was decided to hold off sending the army onto the island for now. The big bosses just wanna keep observing the test subjects and see what happens. Same goes for the refugee women and the baby. Rescue's outta the question for the time being, at least until The Machine has been stabilised. Scary business.

Journal entry dated 9th Jan 2018.

***

Cynthia's head was still spinning from the bizarre events of the night just gone when she all but fell through the door of her crummy Tempe apartment (which had been far from crummy when she moved in). She fed her big ginger tomcat Mashed Potato, sat with him a while, smoothing and playing with him. Then she tossed aside her specs and crashed out on her (unmade) bed for a few hours' sleep. Later, she would be meeting up with some friends for a lunchtime drink at the Rockingbird Bar. Later arrived sooner than she'd have liked.

"Hey, Cynth," said Heather.

They shared a quick hug before slumping down into their seats.

"Aren't you hot?" Cynthia asked her friend.

"Why thank you," Heather said with a flick of her purple dreads, "I guess I am."

"I meant in a leather jacket. So warm in here."

"Nah. I'm good. It's always the weather for leather."

"So how's the biz treating ya?"

There was a tight and vibrant music scene in Scottsdale and all the musos knew and supported each other. Indeed, it was how Cynthia, Heather and Matt had all met. As teenagers, they had all played together in a hardcore band called God I Hate You. Matt had come up with the name and it was a pretty cool one, Cynthia had to admit. But disaster struck when Heather and Matt became 'a thing'. When band members become 'a thing', Cynthia knew, it invariably meant the end was nigh. And so it turned out to be. Heather and Matt split up which in turn meant God I Hate You split up. Then Matt met someone else, liked it, put a ring on it and went on to have to have two crazy little boys. So now Heather played lead in a nu-metal band called Dusty Hand Turkey. Cynthia thought this was the worst band name she'd ever heard, but she kept that to herself.

"Our manager thinks he can get us a slot at UFest, "Heather replied with a wide smile.

"You're shitting me! Aren't Five Finger Death Punch headlining?"

"Yeah. Cool, right? Nice shirt, by the way."

Today, Cynthia was sporting a Megadeth shirt. She entertained daydreams about bumping into their bassist when out and about in Scottsdale so she always wore one just in case. Then she spied Alison's coat draped over the back of a third seat.

"She's getting the drinkies in," Heather said, as if reading her friend's mind.

"Hi, Cynthia. You look dreadful."

Alison, the Al in question, had appeared carrying three bottles; two beers for her friends and a mineral water for herself. There was something almost motherly about the way she spoke to Cynthia and she always used her full name.

"Hey, Al. Great to see you too."

Another hug was shared, this one a little longer-lasting, and also a peck on the cheek.

"Didn't you shower before you came out?" Alison asked, her nose crinkling.

"No. Didn't have time after I woke up."

"And you couldn't have set your alarm for ten

minutes earlier?"

"I didn't set an alarm."

"In which case, you're only here out of pure luck."

"Pretty much. Mashed Potato says hi, by the way."

"Oh, good. I do miss Mashed Potato. How is he?"

"Same as always. Still master of his domain."

"Wait a sec," interrupted Heather. "Are you guys on or off now? I'm confused."

"Off," Cynthia and Alison replied in unison.

"Okay. Just wanted to be clear."

Alison was Cynthia's on/off girlfriend, but lately more off than on. Despite this, Heather couldn't help noticing that Alison's eyes stayed fixed on Cynthia. But anyway, down to business.

"So, what's this 'hot shit' you've got for us?" Heather asked.

This being a Tuesday afternoon, and an early one at that, the bar still wasn't busy. In fact, it was barely ticking over. But there was muted conversation from the handful of other patrons and relatively quiet music from the retro jukebox. Old time rock n roll, as Bob Seger had put it.

"Ladies," Cynthia began with a smile as she theatrically pushed her glasses up the bridge of her nose, "I have hot shit in all kinds of flavours and all kinds of colours. Prepare yourself for a tale of…"

"Cynthia, please," Alison sighed with a roll of her eyes. "Just get on with it."

"Okay okay. So, two days ago, something big went

down at the port and none of us knew what, but there were suits rushing around like World War Three had come early or something. It was in a lab on an island off the east coast of Africa. Officially, it's R 'n D for…"

"R 'n D?" Heather queried.

"Research and development," Alison offered.

"Yeah, research and development," Cynthia confirmed. "So, officially it's R 'n D for the commercial space flights which still haven't happened. I don't know what they do there exactly, I just watch the doors and service elevator, you know."

"Sounds amazing," Heather said with a pinch of sarcasm. "Any jobs going?"

"Put a lid on it. So, on Sunday something went wrong like King Kong and all these suits from Central Security hit panic-mode and start rushing around. Next thing, we're ushered into this conference room and this dude called Neal Terry, who I've seen around, tells us that the lab is *actually* being used for prepping astronauts for long distance space travel, like to Mars and stuff."

"Whoah!" gasped Heather.

"I know, right? And he says they've been adapting the astronauts' bodies so they can survive stasis, suspended animation, but while they were in their pods – you know, stasis pods – there was a malfunction, something to do with a hurricane that hit Madagascar, and their brains got turned to mush."

"Jesus!" Heather gasped. "That's gross!"

Alison looked like she was concentrating hard. "Go

on," she said.

"And then he tells us as a result of all these body modifications they're now all seven feet tall, hairless and blue."

Heather threw herself back into her seat. "What the actual fuck?"

"We're telling you this in case you see any of them on your monitors, he said."

"And did you?" Alison asked.

"I did," Cynthia confirmed. "A ship was wrecked in this hurricane and a bunch of refugees made it ashore on a lifeboat and got attacked by these blue dudes, because they're now all, like, savages. Apparently, it was carnage. But there were two women and a baby that managed to get away, and they found their way to the emergency door that I monitor. I had to let them in before two of these blue dudes ripped them to shreds."

"Fuuuuck."

Alison had been storing up a bank of questions. "So…"

"Hang on. I haven't got to the really weird shit yet. So then, yesterday, I swear to god, two fucking Men in Black – well, actually it was a man and a woman in black – came to see me at work. But they were only dressed up like the Men in Black because I saw them both at the airport before that and they were dressed normal. They tell me they're from the CI fucking A and they want me to work with them in the 'top tier' to try and sort all this mess out. And get this, their names were

Al Leon, like 'alien', and Champagne Star, like she's a fucking porn star or something."

"Man, that's the craziest shit ever!"

"Yeah. Insane."

Alison was wearing her 'thinking face'. It was a face Cynthia knew well.

"Uh oh. Looks like the professor is formulating a theory," Heather chuckled before taking a swig from her bottle.

Alison was academic by nature. She lived to learn. In this respect, she was the complete opposite of Cynthia. Alison had majored in anthropology. Cynthia had majored in heavy metal theory. Alison was hyper-aware of societal trends and patterns of behaviour. Cynthia could explain to you the shades of difference between hard rock and heavy metal, between death metal and Norwegian black metal.

Their circle of friends, and indeed their families, had been surprised when they had hooked up. Sure, they were both great looking in completely different ways; Cynthia, ever pale and pasty, with her horn-rimmed glasses, mohawk and tattoos. And Alison, mixed race, with her chic outfits and halo of curls, worn in honour of her idol Whitney Houston. Also, Cynthia revelled in her slobbishness, eating hot dogs for breakfast and crashing out in her clothes, while Alison went running every morning and ate seeds, something Cynthia found completely baffling.

"Aren't you supposed to wait till they grow into

something first?" she'd ask.

However, despite these differences, things had gone great, just as Alison had always predicted.

"You're Aquarius," she had explained to a cynical Cynthia. "I'm Aries. We're compatible."

Even Alison's conservative parents had embraced their daughter's new partner. And why? Because Cynthia brought the fun. When Alison had introduced her to them, they had looked her up and down through panic-stricken eyes. Who was this tattooed punk girl? What is our beloved daughter playing at? But, one informal lunch later, they had completely fallen for her. Cynthia emanated fun in dangerously high doses, and resistance was futile.

But eventually, Cynthia's unfaltering dedication to slobbishness had proven too much for Alison and they parted ways, at least for a little while. And so the ritual of splitting up/getting back together had begun.

'I Was Made for Loving You' by Kiss came on the jukebox and Alison turned to Cynthia. "You know what's going on here, right?" she asked.

"Yeah. Kiss's biggest selling single."

"I'm talking about the spaceport."

"No. I haven't a fucking clue," Cynthia stated matter-of-factly.

"It's misinformation," said Alison.

"Hey, I've got their first album," Heather interjected with a grin.

"Shut up, Heather," Cynthia said. "I wanna hear

this."

Alison took a deep breath and delivered what could only be described as a thesis: "Not only do we now live in a post-truth world, we live in a post-secret world. Thanks to the internet, specifically social media, it's impossible to keep anything secret anymore. Everything's going to come out, no matter what. People can't help themselves. Sharing is now their default reaction to everything. So what can governments and corporations do to cover stuff up when it's pretty much guaranteed to make it out into the public sphere? Simple: drown it in misinformation." She regarded Cynthia through narrowed eyes. "And you, missy, have played right into their hands."

"Exsqueeze me?"

"You've just become a part of their misinformation machine."

"Oh?"

"Somewhere further on down the line, what happened on this island is inevitably going to come out. There'll be footage of these blue men online, rampaging around, or testimonies from monitors such as yourself saying this happened and that happened. News of these long-distance space missions will also come out, but it'll all be surrounded by accompanying stories of Men in Black with ridiculous names, of CIA involvement, and it'll all sound unbelievable, because of all the bullshit they've concocted around it. The bullshit you've already started spreading. Don't you see?"

"Actually, yeah. Kind of."

"And I guarantee you this, there'll be plenty more to come. The bullshit machine is just warming up. Soon they'll be manufacturing tonnes of it, so no one will be able to differentiate between what's true and what isn't."

Heather lifted her bottle up as if making a toast. "Think I'll stick with music, thanks all the same," she said.

Cynthia looked downtrodden. "I gotta say, I feel kinda depressed after hearing that."

"Don't be," said Alison between sips from her bottle of water. "If they're offering you more money along with this promotion, then take it. Just be aware. Recognise the bullshit when it's presented to you. Call it out. You're smart. You'll know if someone tries taking you for a ride."

"You really think I'm smart?"

"I absolutely think you're smart."

"Well, I'll drink to that."

Cynthia clinked her bottle with Alison who in turn clinked with Heather who then clinked with Cynthia.

"Just keep us informed," Alison said. "Sounds like things are going to get very interesting."

Chapter 11

The apex of the hill, which curiously seemed to be composed entirely of earth and small stones, offered Vital a three-hundred-and-sixty-degree view of the island on which he was trapped. The rain was easing off now and the grey clouds were dissipating. Did that mean the snakes would come slithering out of their hidey-holes again, or were they all just waiting for him at the foot of the hill? He felt Walter standing with him, just behind his left shoulder. He looked but his friend was not there. And then the rain was gone.

"Oh, Walter."

He felt that he owed it to his football-mad companion to escape this accursed island. To survive in Walter's honour. But then what? To return to Burundi to explain to Walter's parents what had happened to their son? To see out their plan by continuing on to Manchester in far-away England? It occurred to him that he was actually further away from Manchester now than he had been back home.

What were we thinking? the voice inside his head

asked. *We're just boys. Boys with a stupid idea that we never thought through. And now Walter is gone.*

His wet t-shirt and jeans felt cool against his skin. Relishing this reprieve from the stifling humidity, he looked up and through a gap in the retreating clouds saw a plane. It was barely more than a speck in the sky, leaving a thin white vapour trail behind it. Vital longed to be up there, above the clouds, sitting in the well-appointed fuselage of a passenger jet, possibly sipping a coke, eyeing up the air hostesses. He had never been on a plane. He wondered if he'd ever get the chance.

He scanned the horizon and saw a ship, far out. Then he spied another vessel. It seemed to be in the same vicinity as the first one. And then he spotted what could only be a cruise liner. All three boats were spread out on the horizon in a line.

Madagascar must be that way, he thought. *Why else would there be a cruise ship?*

His eyes slipped across the terrain of his new, but hopefully temporary, home. He noticed that the jungle occupied about half the island with a finger of it stretching around the arc of the coast.

That's where we came ashore.

Then something far across the plain caught his eye. It was hard to make out, but it looked like a huddle of buildings, but not the ruined ones he'd just spent the night in. There was a dome, a big one, and a satellite dish, also huge. A thought occurred, and an exciting one at that.

I wonder if those sisters are there.

From his vantage point he traced the line of his and Walter's mad dash across the plain and figured the sisters would have been heading roughly in the direction of this mysterious site. His heart began thumping in his chest, not with fear, but with hope.

If they are there, I will find them, and we can all get off this island together.

Then he noticed that two of the blue savages, still like tiny ants from this far away, had re-emerged from the jungle and were now between the hill he was standing on and the compound, the place he had resolved to get to. But that was okay because his spirits had lifted, his resolve had strengthened and his brain had kicked into high gear. He had a plan, and a quite brilliant one too, or so he thought. And so Vital began his descent from the hill, towards the hungry snakes and the blue savages.

***

Earlier, Esperance and Godriva had stood huddled together under a large sun umbrella on the roof of the living block watching the blue men fleeing from the rain and thunder.

"Look at them," Godriva had observed with a sneer. "A bit of rain and they are like little children."

It had been a frustrating morning for the sisters and they had both welcomed the rain as it brought with it relief from the oppressive humidity. Now, in the cool aftermath of the downpour, Esperance was sitting cross-legged on the floor surrounded by the technical manuals she had retrieved from the various bunkrooms.

On a nearby lounger, Buki was sleeping next to his mother who was playing with her newly acquired Nintendo Switch. Suddenly, the noises from her device ceased and she sat up.

"They're coming back," she said.

"The blue men?"

"Yes."

Esperance sighed. "You'd think they'd have learned by now, they're not going to get in."

"I know."

Only a tiny portion of Esperance's brain was engaging with Godriva. The rest of it was grappling with the concepts laid out in impenetrable language and complex graphs in the technical manuals. However, Esperance was understanding enough of it to have her grim suspicions about the origins of the blue men sadly confirmed.

...victims of acute trauma have been placed into suspended animation for short periods. Known as Emergency Preservation and Resuscitation (EPR), the technique involves cooling the subject to between 10°c and 15°c by replacing their blood with frozen saline. EPR offers doctors an extended period of time in which to...

...the arctic ground squirrel has been known to survive for up to nine months in a frozen state, apparently suffering no ill effects when thawing out. This is because of the absence of ice nucleators in its blood. Without the nucleators, ice cannot form...

...replacing the body's water with as much saline as possible is vital if the subject is to survive the freezing process with their organs intact. Also, the introduction of a synthesised glycerol is necessary during the...

...in order to increase red blood cell production and encourage cognitive regeneration, erythropoietin and modafinil are to be introduced to the test subjects during the gene editing phase of the process...

It was the bit about gene editing that switched the light on in Esperance's mind. She tossed away the manual that had been open on her lap. Her body felt stiff so she stretched her arms over her head, causing her elbows to crack loudly.

"Ouch!" said Godriva on her sister's behalf. "That didn't sound good."

Esperance let out a long sigh and broached the subject she had been dreading.

"I think they were made here."

"What were?"

"Not what. Who. The blue men."

A dark cloud fell over Godriva. "Sister, are you

serious?"

"Yes. I think they were experimented on, like lab rats."

"But why?"

"Who knows? But these are all SpaceWurd manuals, so it must be something to do with going into space. Perhaps they were being prepared for something but it went wrong. I don't think they were supposed to turn out the way they did. But this manual..." Esperance held it up, "...explains how it was all done. It talks about rewriting the genetic code. It's got pages and pages describing cocktails of drugs, some of which I've never heard of. What mixes of drugs are administered when, into which parts of the body. It's been going on for a couple of years, according to this."

"So cruel."

"If the blue men were astronauts, then they'd have volunteered, put themselves forward. I think they were supposed to go into space for a very long time. It's an incredibly complicated process. Very cutting edge."

"Sound's horrible," Godriva murmured, her mouth forming a snarl.

"Also, there's one manual for male test subjects and another one for female, but all the blue people we've seen are male. What happened to all the women?"

"Probably the same thing that happens to women everywhere else in the world," said Godriva.

Esperance looked up to see that the sun was peeking out from behind the thinning clouds. She rubbed her eyes which were now sore after all that reading and studying. The gentle swishing of the waves on the distant beach drifted through the haze to her ears. The sound was soothing, cooling.

"This island," she said. "Nice place for a visit, but I wouldn't want to live here."

Buki scrunched up his face – a warning sign his mother knew well – and started crying. But was he crying because he was hungry, because he was tired or because he was trapped in a compound surrounded by giant blue savages? Who could tell? Here, on this island, the usual order of things had been violently disrupted.

"He's awake," Godriva said. "We have disturbed him."

She lifted the t-shirt she had liberated from an abandoned bunkroom and put Buki to her breast.

"You aren't wearing your sling," Esperance observed.

Godriva windmilled her shoulder. "The sling was a pain and it itched. I'm better off without it."

Esperance smiled. "As your nurse, I insist that you..."

"You're not on duty now, sister," Godriva said coldly.

***

As expected, the snakes started emerging from their hidey-holes as soon as he approached the foot of the earthy hill. This time, however, Vital was not afraid.

"Come on then," he urged, slowing down so as to give them a sporting chance of catching him.

Once again, the ground all but came alive. In less than a minute, a squirming carpet of hungry reptiles was writhing towards him, hissing, jumping and nipping. He felt several sharp pinches through his jeans and backed away before turning to run for the desiccated tree that had earlier given him sanctuary.

The backs of his legs were smarting by the time he scrambled up to the safety of the high branches. His mind flashed back to that moment the previous year when he had visited a market to buy jeans. Which to choose, the cheap pair by some company he'd never heard of or the genuine Levi's? Flush with the first wages from his new safari park job, he had plumped for the Levi's. Boy, was he glad now that he had.

It occurred to him then that Walter had been with him that day. Walter, who never wore jeans, only shorts. Walter, Walter, Walter. It seemed now that every memory Vital carried around in his head had some connection to his lost friend. He wondered what Walter would have made of this crazy plan of his. Speaking of which, it was time to put the next stage of it into action.

He squinted through the shimmering afternoon air towards the compound. The sun was at its zenith in the sky, baking the ground and evaporating the rainwater that had earlier fallen. He was pretty sure he could still see only two of the blue savages out on the plain. His heart began pounding. Was he really going to do this? With thousands of snakes writhing around below him, he didn't really have a choice. Ah, well. Best to just get it over and done with.

He drew in a deep breath and yelled as loud as he could: "HEEEEELLLLOOOOO!" And then he did it again. And again. And again.

He wasn't even sure if the blue savages would hear him from such a distance, but he was hopeful that the still air would carry his cries far across the flat terrain and to their ears. What Vital could not know was that, as part of their body modifications, the test subjects had had their hearing capabilities enhanced. When these mysterious faraway shouts reached them, the blue men turned and with their augmented sight spotted the source. The one thought that flashed collectively across their minds was experienced as a concept rather than a word, and it was: 'prey'.

Vital began to have second thoughts about this plan of his when he saw the two blue dots sprinting towards him at a speed that could only be described as inhuman. He realised that he had not stopped to consider that, as well as being freakishly tall, they might have other extraordinary physical attributes. Their blue skin could, for example, be impenetrable, which would mean he was in very serious trouble.

Despite the considerable distance already covered, there was no sign of any slackening in the blue savages' pace. In fact, the closer they got to Vital and his precious tree the faster they seemed to be moving. Or was that just an optical illusion? Either way, it was extremely disconcerting.

They are like superhumans, Vital thought. This was followed by, *Oh god, what have I done?*

They were close now, close enough for Vital to discern the details of their bodies; their elongated limbs, their hairless heads, their swinging penises. Vital was not someone who habitually preyed, but right now he was directing pleas to an unspecified god somewhere in the sky above. *Please let this work! Please, please, please let this work!*

With their yellow eyes locked onto the boy in the tree, the blue savages pounded onward, each foot strike sending a tiny shockwave through the ground like a ripple on the surface of a pond. These ripples were felt by the morass of snakes that were slithering around the base of the tree like a great, reptilian whirlpool, and it precipitated a change in their collective behaviour.

Vital watched in horrified fascination as the snakes melted away into the rocky crevices and hidey-holes.

"What? No! Come back!" he jabbered dumbly as his great plan seemed to come undone. "Come back! Come back!"

The two savages reached the foot of the hill. Vital closed his eyes. *I'm dead,* he thought. His muscles slackened as he accepted the inevitable. All he could do was wait and hope it would be over quickly. But with his eyes closed, Vital did not see the miracle that then occurred. It was only when the blue savages started yelping and crying out that he dared to look again, and what he saw was a multitude of blue limbs thrashing desperately around in a sea of reptiles.

The snakes, it transpired, were ambush predators. Upon sensing the approaching prey they had slithered away to lie in wait. Once their prey was in the centre of their web, as it were, they engulfed it.

The writhing bodies of the savages appeared to have sucked up all the snakes from the immediate surroundings, and Vital could not imagine a more awful death; slow, agonising and nightmarish. The savages had become the savaged, and Vital had a feeling Walter would have approved.

He squinted across the plain. There was no sign of any more savages which meant that his path was clear. Vital gingerly shimmied down the petrified trunk, turned his back on the painful screams of his would-be killers, and crept away. No snakes came slithering after him and he felt no nips at the back of his legs. It was only when he was about halfway across the plain on his way to the compound that, with cold horror, he realised his plan hadn't been quite as fool proof as he'd thought.

***

Esperance paced the perimeter fence like a caged gazelle. Back home in Bujumbura she had been a gifted runner, and so had her sister. As girls they had ran for

114

their school and, often, they had won. In fact, they had won often enough for there to be talk of a 'career' for the both of them. Their mother dreamed of the gold medals waiting to be scooped up by these two lightning-fast sisters from Burundi. The marathons of the world were theirs for the taking. But for Godriva, these great plans and schemes had come to a screeching halt with her unexpected pregnancy. In sisterly solidarity, Esperance had slipped off her running shoes too, but now she was feeling the pull again.

A calling always calls loudest when it's beyond reach, and the one thing Esperance wanted to do most of all right now, she couldn't. She didn't want to run away, just to run. Run for the sheer joy of it. She yearned to unleash the fearsome potential of her leg muscles and tear across the plain in wild abandon, but beyond the protection of the stainless-steel fence was certain death, and so she remained caged.

She wrapped her fingers around the links and stared out at the world beyond. *I have been still for too long,* she thought. *No matter where we end up, back home or in South Africa, I will run again.* And then something caught her eye. At first she thought it must be one of the blue savages, but no, she was quite sure now that it wasn't. And if it wasn't one of the blue savages, it could only be…

Esperance called to her sister up on the living block roof. "Godriva! Godriva!"

But Godriva did not hear her sister's cries, for she

was asleep, and dreaming…

Four months into the pregnancy – not even halfway! – Godriva reads that she should start speaking to her developing baby who can now apparently hear. She struggles with this concept. This growing bump feels alien, as if it's not actually a part of her but instead some sort of aberration.

Fast forward.

When Bukeneza eventually decides it's time to leave, Godriva enters the hospital without the father but with every intention of accepting every single drug offered to her. She is numb and she wants to stay that way.

Fast forward.

A baby, it seems, does not come as a single self-contained unit. When Godriva, drunk from a swirling cocktail of pure love and maternal terror, walks through the front door of her family home, she does so with not just a baby in tow, but also a bewildering array of accessories, paraphernalia, pamphlets and advice. She feels overwhelmed, as if she is drowning in a sea of responsibility. She is overcome with an urge that often falls upon her when she feels herself to be out of her depth: to disappear.

Fast forward.

All the pamphlets in the world could not have prepared Godriva, or her body, for the amount of feeding this little baby requires. It is mind-boggling, exhausting and apparently limitless, and she struggles to envisage a life beyond being a human milk bottle.

Fast forward.

Godriva, cut adrift now from her homeland and her home, feels herself becoming hyper-aware of her baby's existence. With every day that passes he becomes less and less an accessory of hers – a thing that requires servicing and maintenance – and more and more a being in his own right. He is developing a personality, and Godriva can quite easily imagine him one day occupying his own space in the world and thriving without her. This makes her feel simultaneously joyous and crushed.

She looks down at him, asleep in the crook of her arm on the lounger. He in turn looks at her, then his eyes come sharply into focus. Godriva feels a chill ripple through her body, just before her baby whispers, "Godriva. Godriva."

Godriva snapped awake. She held her breath and looked around frantically. There was little Buki, still blissfully asleep on the lounger next to her. But where was her sister?

"Godriva! Godriva!"

Godriva jumped up and looked down from the roof of the living block.

"Shush! Buki's sleeping!" she hissed.

"Someone's coming! Look!"

Esperance pointed, Godriva squinted. The rainclouds of that morning had by now dissipated completely, leaving only blue sky, hazy sun and humid heat.

"Oh, god."

"Come down!" Esperance cried. "Bring Buki!"

Two minutes later, Godriva, who was still trying to shake the dream from her mind, came stumbling out through the door with Buki in her arms.

"Can you see who it is? Is it one of the boys from the beach?"

"Could be. Can't tell yet."

Esperance still had her fingers wrapped around the links in the fence. The figure out there on the plain was closer now, and clearer. Whoever it was, they were definitely male, and he was waving his arms around frantically.

"Call that running," Esperance said to no one but herself. "He needs to pick those knees up."

Godriva's fingers wrapped around Esperance's and they exchanged a look. Although they still could not tell who the figure approaching them was, the mere fact of his existence meant that there was hope. It meant they were not alone here after all. It meant that it was possible to survive out there beyond the great, steel fence. It meant that perhaps there were more survivors waiting to be found. It meant that maybe – just maybe – a way off this accursed island was within reach.

The figure was still waving and so Esperance and Godriva waved back. Godriva groaned as she did so.

"Ouch! My arm!"

"I told you. You should be wearing your sling."

"Yes, doctor," Godriva mocked.

"HEEEEYYYY!"

They could hear him now, calling across the plain. They waved and called back.

"It *is* one of those boys from the boat. The ones we saw running away," Godriva said, getting excited.

"Yes. But where's the other one?"

As there was only one possible answer to that question, Godriva said nothing.

"HEEEYYYY!"

"I'll bet he's hungry," Godriva said.

"Not for long," Esperance replied. "We have enough food to feed an army."

Buki, cradled in Godriva's good arm, started crying. It was almost as if he knew something was about to happen. Something bad.

"Shush shush, Buki. It's only…"

The following words were left unspoken. Godriva hadn't noticed it before now, and neither had her sister, but directly behind the approaching boy was a second figure. It was one of the blue savages, hot in pursuit, and he was fast closing the gap.

"Oh. My. God," was all Esperance could say.

"Sister. Look."

Godriva was pointing away in another direction. From the west, a second blue figure was approaching at the speed of a cheetah, leaving a great plume of dust in its wake.

"RUUUUUUUN!" they screamed to the boy. "RUUUUUUUUN!"

Vital, his limbs screaming in pain, could now see the two women beyond the fence jumping up and down, pointing and yelling. And then he saw it, the second blue savage tearing its way across the plain to head him off. No human could run that fast, surely. But then, were these things actually human?

Tears poured down Godriva's face. "RUUUUUUN!" she screamed until her throat was raw. "RUUUUUN!"

By now, Buki too was screaming.

"Take him inside!" Esperance snapped, but Godriva did not move.

"Why is he coming this way?" Godriva cried. "He needs to be going that way!" She pointed in the direction of the trench and its hidden entrance.

But still the boy approached, as fast as his burning legs could carry him.

"THAT WAY!" Esperance shouted, pointing in the opposite direction of the approaching blue savage. "THAT WAY!"

Now Esperance and Godriva could see clearly the

visage of horror that was the boy's face. A moment later, he crashed full speed into the fence, wrapping his fingers around the links. Esperance wrapped her fingers around his, as Godriva had done with hers only moments before. The young man was dirty, sweaty and mad with terror. The look in his eyes screamed out one thing and one thing only: "Help me!"

Godriva stepped back, afraid of what she saw, afraid to be in such close proximity to fear so acute and primal. Esperance pointed to the east, in the direction of the distant rocky outcrop.

"Go that way. You'll see a trench. Jump into it and run back. At the end of the trench is a door. Just hit the keypad and they'll let you in."

"They?"

"GO!"

The boy ran. Seconds later Esperance and Godriva looked on in helpless, horrified awe as the giant blue savage sprinted past, in pursuit, at a truly incredible speed.

***

Ed had spent his entire professional life operating under a misapprehension. He believed that in order to work one's way up the greasy career pole, one had to ingratiate oneself with the people above you, with one's superiors. And the way one did this, Ed believed, was by snitching on people. That he had so far only managed to shimmy up to the relatively lowly position of Monitoring Station Supervisor, Ed did not accept as evidence that his understanding of the mechanics of career enhancement was flawed. On the contrary, he saw it as evidence that he had simply not snitched enough.

He was completely wrong in this belief, of course, for this one very simple reason: no 'superior' was ever going to promote a snitch because at some point that snitch might start snitching on them. One day, Ed might have come to realise this himself, but today was not that day, and so he had just snitched on Matt.

Earlier, he had happened to find himself behind Matt in the disorderly queue to clock in. Out of nothing more than idle curiosity, Ed had peaked over Matt's shoulder to see how much flexitime he had accrued. He hadn't actually been looking for a reason to snitch on him, he just wanted to know if Matt had managed to harvest more flexitime than himself. It turns out Matt had, which made Ed angry.

Also, there was something else at play. Matt was friends with that dyke bitch Cynthia, the waster who had leapfrogged Ed to a cushy position in the top tier. And so, in order to take a strike at Cynthia, Ed had snitched on Matt.

This had resulted in Matt receiving an email from their line manager:

Hey Matt. I see you've built up quite a bit of flexi

there. Might want to think about taking some time off, dude. Clive.

To this, Matt had replied:

Hey Clive. Sure. No probs. Matt.

What Ed was blissfully ignorant of was that Matt and Clive were buddies, having bonded over a shared love of all things *Star Wars*. They would occasionally meet up outside work and debate the finer points of the *Han Solo at Stars' End* novel published in 1979, or attempt to decipher what the hell Palpatine's plan was exactly in *The Phantom Menace*. But whereas Matt was just your average *Star Wars* geek, Clive was a self-confessed superfan. Look closely at his tie, for example, and one would see that it was patterned with interlocking Naboo starfighters. Catch a glimpse of his socks and one would notice that they were adorned with little R2-D2s. His jacket bore Darth Vader cufflinks. His wristwatch flashed an *Attack of the Clones* logo.

Clive was such a superfan, in fact, that he had actually started penning his autobiography, detailing his passion for all things Force-related. It was titled: 'Mint, Unopened: My Love Affair with Licensed Products.'

Ed had spent his entire shift so far sitting at the workstation adjacent to Matt, the one recently vacated by Cynthia, for whom he was covering until a replacement could be found. This had also helped to stoke the fire that was now raging inside his guts. He had been studying Matt, waiting for some tell-tale sign that his snitching had yielded the desired result. But no tell-tale sign had yet come; no flicker across the face, no hushed curse words. In fact, Matt seemed to be in a remarkably chirpy mood, which only served to further provoke Ed's ire. He was approaching breaking point now and was ready to lash out, to punish, to hurt.

At that very moment, half a world away, Vital was leaping into a trench, the one Esperance in her tearful desperation had directed him to. With the two blue savages closing fast, he changed direction and began the sprint back towards the compound. Above the sound of his panting, he heard the THUD of his pursuers hitting the ground somewhere behind him. The trench suddenly became a tunnel with green lights below and white lights above. Up ahead he could see a huge, steel door. Above it and to the right was the keypad the beautiful sister had told him about. He glanced back over his shoulder. The blue savages were still after him but they had lost their speed. They were too tall for the tunnel and were now approaching on all fours.

Ed suddenly sat bolt upright. There was a black kid running towards the emergency door at the east Africa site, the one everything had kicked off at a few days ago. And, Christ! There were a couple of those blue test subjects Neal Terry had told them to look out for! Ed slyly peaked to his right. Matt had his eyes on his own screens and hadn't noticed the drama unfolding on his neighbour's. The black kid was almost at the door now. Ed could see the look of rampant terror on his face. The kid started jabbing at the keypad, and so Ed blanked the screen, pulled out his SmartCard and went to make himself a coffee.

***

Esperance was in the airlock, pacing. Godriva was standing high above her, looking down through the hatch.

"Can you hear anything?" she called down.

"No. Nothing. I don't like this."

"Surely he should be there by now. Why haven't they let him in?"

Esperance pressed her ear up against the door. "Oh, this is ridiculous!" she snapped. "What's happened?"

Godriva started to look uneasy. "You don't think…?"

"No. Surely they wouldn't just leave him to be…you know. Go and see if you can see anything out there, on the plain."

With Buki sitting uncomfortably in the crook of her good arm, Godriva trotted over to the fence and peered through the heat-haze.

"Esperance!" she yelled. "Esperance! Come!"

Esperance abandoned her vigil by the steel door, shot up the entire length of the ladder faster than a squirrel climbs a tree and sprinted over to her sister.

"Look!"

The blue savages who had pursued Vital into the trench had reappeared. One was standing in the sun while the other was hauling himself out of the trench. Even from such a distance it was easy to see they were both covered in blood.

"Oh no," murmured Esperance.

One of the blue savages stretched his limbs before sloping off in the direction of the jungle at a lazy pace. His fellow pack member soon followed.

"They didn't let him in," a shocked and shaken Godriva stammered.

Esperance recognised the warning signs in the way only a big sister could. "Godriva. It's okay. Sit down. Breathe."

"They didn't let him in."

"Here. Give Buki to me."

"They didn't let him in."

Esperance took Buki from Godriva who was fast careering towards a breakdown.

"They didn't let him in. They didn't let him in. They didn't let him in!"

And then Godriva realised, somewhat darkly, that it was with her pregnancy that this chain of catastrophic events had begun; the escape from Burundi, the shipwreck, the blue savages, the boy who had just died. Did that fact make all this Buki's fault, or hers? Or perhaps it was Benjamin's. If she'd never met him then she never would have fallen pregnant and he might never have been killed and she would have had no reason to run away. But then, it was Esperance who had introduced them, so…

This train of thought was leading her to a very grim place. Walls were closing in on her. The ground was swallowing her up. Devils were chanting in her ears. She broke into a sprint and with the speed of a train she raced around the inside perimeter of the great steel fence, screaming at the heavens as she went.

***

With coffee in hand, Ed returned to his seat. Matt gave him a polite nod as he sat down and went back to his work. Ed didn't return it. He was still simmering over his neighbour apparently getting away with building up too much flexi and with Cynthia getting away with merely existing. He took a sip from his steaming Americano with a splash of hot milk, just the way he liked it, and slipped his SmartCard back into his machine. What flashed up on the screen was the POV from the cam in the emergency tunnel at the east Africa site. It showed the eviscerated remains of a young man spread all over the walls like strawberry jam.

"Whoah! What the hell?"

Matt had seen it! Ed yanked the SmartCard from the machine as the enormity of what he had done crashed down on him like a bloody tidal wave.

"Dude! Put that back in!" Matt demanded.

Ed looked at him as a deer in a trap would look at its killer. "It's nothing…go back to your…"

"There was a fucking dead guy on your screen!"

Colleagues, alerted by Matt's outburst and shocked by his rare use of the f-word, rushed over.

"What's going on?" asked one.

Ed stood up and tried to pull rank. "If you could all just return to your stations, please."

"There was a fucking dead guy on his screen and he took his SmartCard out!" Matt stated loudly and clearly for all to hear.

All Ed could do in response was mumble and stammer, "No…no I didn't…you are clearly mistaken…"

"Mistaken, my ass! Put your card back in!"

Then Neal Terry appeared looking monumentally pissed off and Ed entered his own personal ninth circle of hell. His downfall was being played out in real time, in front of all the people he had, at one time or another, snitched on.

Neal marched right up to the slimy little creep who nobody liked until he was nose-to-nose with him. "You are in so much fucking trouble," he rumbled.

Chapter 12

"How are you feeling now? Any better?"

Godriva did not answer. She did not even move. She was lying in the foetal position on a lounger on the living block roof, shielded from the worst of the late afternoon sun by a large umbrella.

"Are you going to eat something? I can fetch you some cereal if you like."

Esperance was extremely worried about her sister. She had seen Godriva break down before, but never like this. This was deep. Godriva was hurting and hurting bad. Esperance tried a different tack.

"Buki needs his dinner too. Do you want me to bring him over for you?"

Still nothing. Esperance started stroking Godriva's arm.

"When you're ready to talk about it, sister, I'll be here. It always helps to talk."

That the boy had died mere feet from Esperance, with only a steel door between them, was not an easy thing to compartmentalise. In trying to help him, Esperance and Godriva had guided him to his death. It was yet another horror chalked up against them by this island of nightmares.

And then, finally, Godriva spoke. "We're going to die in here," she mumbled.

It was not what Esperance was hoping to hear from her despairing sister, but at least it was something.

"That's up to us. If we don't give up, then we won't die."

Godriva turned over and looked Esperance in the eye. "How can you say that after everything that's happened? This place is...unnatural. People like us aren't meant to be here. It's cursed."

Esperance tried her best to stay calm. "I'm not going to listen to any more talk like that. Every nightmare we've encountered here is man-made. We can survive this if we stay strong. We just have to keep our eyes open for the right opportunity. If this experience has taught me anything it's that you never know what tomorrow might bring."

Had Esperance any inkling of what tomorrow did actually have in store for her, she would have shrivelled up into a ball alongside her sister and cried. But for now, the tension was eased by a loud rumble from the direction of Godriva's stomach.

"See?" said Esperance with a little smile. "I knew you must be hungry. Are you sure you don't want me to fix you a little something?"

Godriva's tears had stopped flowing but her eyes

were still red and raw. "Well, maybe a little something," she conceded.

Esperance leaned in and hugged Godriva close.

"One day, all this will be just a bad memory. You'll see."

Godriva hugged her back.

"I hope so."

Esperance departed for the kitchen, leaving her sister to feed Buki. By the time she returned with a tray laden with far more than 'a little something', evening was creeping over the island. The birds in the distant jungle had ceased their cawing for the night, so the sisters ate their meals in comfortable silence, each grateful for the other's company and for the warm embrace of a hot meal.

"How was your food?" Esperance asked.

Godriva scrunched her nose up. "Hm. Okay. Everything here is so…western."

They had dined on cheeseburgers and fries. The burgers, which came packaged in their buns, had been microwaved. The fries had also been microwaved. Indeed, most of the food in the storeroom was of the microwavable variety.

"American facility," Esperance shrugged. "Just going to have to rough it, I'm afraid."

"What wouldn't I give for some marahagwe?" Godriva said with a lick of the lips. "The peaches were nice, though."

In addition to all the microwavable convenience food

down in the storeroom there was lots of tinned fruit. This had come as a great relief to Esperance as it meant that neither she or her sister would catch scurvy.

Esperance laid back and gazed up at the deep blue heavens. "The stars," she said, "so bright."

"You can see the Milky Way again. Look," Godriva quietly said.

A band of twinkling stars wrapped in a gaseous swathe snaked its intergalactic way across the sky, fading in and then back out without kissing either horizon.

"So clear," said Godriva. "It doesn't look real."

"I have to get a picture."

Esperance reached for her phone which was on the floor next to her lounger. As she did so, something moved into view overhead, something that had no business being there.

"Esperance," Godriva breathed, "do you see that?"

Esperance retrieved her phone, laid back on her sun lounger and gazed up. She inhaled sharply and attempted to articulate what she was looking at. "It's...it's..."

Godriva stepped in to help. "It's a planet."

"A planet," Esperance agreed. "But not one of ours."

In the darkening evening sky above them, and framed with iridescent stars, a planet had presented itself. It had drifted slowly in from the cosmic periphery and was now hanging over the two sisters fully formed, fully visible. The bulk of the planet's body was of a feint purple hue, with a slightly lighter crescent curving around the side as it reflected the sun.

Godriva whispered, "What is going on?"

Esperance could not answer. All she could do was stare. She had noticed something else, something that was making the fine hairs on the back of her neck prickle. She felt everything she thought she knew about the universe and her place within it crumble into nothingness.

Godriva, sensing that something had changed within her sister, looked warily over to her and asked, "Esperance? What is it?"

Esperance raised a trembling hand and pointed at the planet. "Look," she breathed. "Do you see? Lights."

Godriva squinted. Visible, just barely, in the shadowed portion of the planet's body, were cobweb-thin patterns of yellow light, spreading out across the surface from central points.

"They look like...cities."

"There's life on that world," Esperance fearfully stated. "There's life on that world right there, right now. We're not alone."

"Oh god," Godriva whispered. She picked her sleeping baby up and held him to her heart. "What is happening here?"

"I have an idea...a theory..."

But the universe was not done with Esperance and Godriva just yet, and so it hurled across the galaxy one more cosmic surprise for them. An electrical distortion began sparking in the immeasurable space between the sisters and the mysterious purple planet which was still hanging full-bodied in the starry sky above them. It was circular, this distortion, and it heralded the arrival of something huge and unnatural.

"Esperance. I'm frightened."

Esperance reached across and squeezed her sister's hand.

The distortion spun like a roman candle, sending out sparks and crackles of lightening. And then *it* appeared; a spaceship, huge, ring-shaped, a grey shade or two off white. There were markings on it, and lights, visible even from this unimaginable distance. Its ring-shaped shadow fell upon the surface of the purple planet.

"It's a spaceship," Esperance breathlessly uttered. "And it's *massive...*"

Godriva looked to her sister and nodded at the thing she was limply holding in her hand: her phone. Dumbly, shakily, Esperance raised it and started recording. A moment or two after the little red dot appeared on the screen, something else happened. A laser, green and intense, shot out from the empty space in the middle of the ring-shaped spacecraft. Then the immense ship started moving slowly along the beam of the laser, which disappeared in its wake. The craft picked up speed, following the beam across the star-sprinkled sky. Then it left the cosmic stage and faded from view.

After a long pause, heavy with dread, Godriva whispered, "You can stop recording now."

Esperance tapped the screen and lowered the phone.

"Please tell me you got that," said Godriva.

"I did."

"Good, because no one would ever believe it otherwise."

Esperance did not respond. She just continued to lie back on her lounger, staring up at the sky. The alien planet, for that is what it was, was still hanging over them.

Without taking her eyes from it, Godriva quietly asked, "Sister. What is your theory?"

Esperance also spoke without taking her eyes from the heavens above. "These past few evenings, we've sat out here looking up at the stars, saying how bright they are, how intense. Well, I don't think they're our stars."

"Not our stars?"

"I think we've been looking at someone else's stars. Stars from far away in space."

Godriva nodded. "Mmm," was all she could manage.

"And what we've just seen, and what we're looking at right now…" she flicked her eyes from the planet to her sister and back again, "…proves it, I think. What that is above us is a window, a window to some other part of the universe, maybe billions of light years away."

The purple planet had almost completed its journey across the hole in the sky now and was fading away. Buki had not seen it. He had slept through the whole thing.

"The question is," Esperance nervously pondered, "if we can see them, does it also mean they can see us?"

Chapter 13

Mr B has begun the process of recruiting new test subjects. Not going to be easy if word of what happened to the last lot gets out. He's moving fast to try and pre-empt that. He's also set up a team to start headhunting replacement scientists and engineers. Not as tall an order as it sounds, actually. Throw the words 'space mission' into the conversation and it's amazing how quickly many of them will drop whatever they're doing and sign up.

Also, the Dowley girl has now been moved to the top tier to help get the facility back online. The plan is to send one of the refugee women down to flick the switch. Needless to say, that'll lead her straight into the path of you-know-who, so things are about to get very interesting.

Journal entry dated 10th January 2018

***

The hills were a gorgeous pale purple under the morning sky and the breeze brought with it the smell of desert sand.

"Hey, Cynth," said Gene. "You look as happy as a hen that just laid an egg."

"Yep," Cynthia confirmed with a smile. "Gimme the most expensive dog on the menu, and half a dozen donuts. I'm celebrating."

"Don't tell me. Yer getting married."

"Hah! No. This is good news. I got me a promotion."

"No shit? Congratulations, Cynth. You can have the donuts on th' house for that."

"Thank you, Gene. You're the best."

"I know. Just don't ferget yer friends when yer heading up the comp'ny."

"Ha ha! No worries there. I'm gonna take you on as my own personal chef."

There were no strangers milling around waiting for the spaceport plane this morning, for which Cynthia was grateful. She'd had quite enough surprises these last few days, thank you very much, even if that last one had turned out to be a hell yeah! Her stomach was jumping now with a cocktail of nervousness and excitement. She had never been down to the top tier before, not even when she'd been given a site tour on her first day. By all accounts, it was sleek, state-of-the-art and sprawling.

She milled around at the back of the queue for the plane, sipping her steaming hot coffee, wondering what the day had in store for her. She'd made no great effort to smarten herself up. She figured they'd want her just the way she was. Besides, as she didn't actually own any smart clothes it's not like they had a choice.

"Hey, Miss High-Flyer!" said Matt as he slipped into the seat next to Cynthia.

"Hey, Matt. How's it going? Missing me yet?"

Matt didn't answer that one and instead issued forth with the good stuff. "You hear about Ed? Hauled off to the top tier by that Neal Terry guy, marched out of the building by security twenty minutes later."

"Fuck off."

"For real. We all knew he was going to screw up eventually, and yesterday was the day."

"Can't believe I wasn't around to see that. Fuck."

"Your language is appalling."

"Yeah," said Cynthia with a shrug. "So go on then. What did the creepy little prick do this time?"

"Killed someone," Matt said flatly.

Cynthia wasn't buying this. No way. "Exsqueeze me?"

"Remember when you let those two girls in through the emergency door at the east Africa site when the blue guys were chasing them?"

"Yeah. Please don't tell me something happened to them."

"Not to them, no. But at the same door at the same site, only this time it was a boy. Blue guys chasing him down, Ed just walked away and left him to die."

Cynthia inhaled sharply. "No. Fucking. Way."

"Way. Saw what was left of him myself when Ed came back. Not going to forget that in a hurry. Someone in top tier clocked that Ed was logged in just before the kid was killed and again just after, so they know what he did."

"That fucking c…"

"I'm telling you, he's finished at SpaceWurd. Career – kaput."

"So is he going to get arrested for that or…?"

"No idea. They'll probably need to arrest him for his own safety. Can you imagine how that wife of his reacted when he told her he'd been fired?"

At this, Cynthia sniggered. "Thought I saw a glow on the horizon last night."

"Yeah. She's a real livewire, apparently. His life's gonna be hell now."

"Good. Don't suppose you took any photos of him being led away."

"No, dammit. Can't believe I didn't think of that."

There were a few moments of silence, and then Cynthia broke it. "Gonna miss you though, dude."

"Yeah, I'm gonna miss you too. There's no one else on the team I can have informed discussions about Megadeth with, that's for sure. How could you do this to me? I thought we were friends?"

"I brought donuts!" Cynthia said with a wicked grin as she held up the bag.

"In that case, I take it all back. You can go, just leave the donuts. Seriously though, do you even know what you're gonna be doing down there?"

"Not a clue. Just hope it's nothing too complex."

***

"We need you to help us stabilise The Machine," said Champagne Star, who was still dressed as a Woman in Black. "When that's done, the facility will be safe and we can send a rescue team in for the refugees."

"If you don't mind me saying so," said Cynthia, "that sounds like a bit of a specialist job. Besides, what's this 'machine'?"

"Once the power's back on, it should be pretty straightforward," Champagne continued, ignoring Cynthia's question. "But in order to do it, we need the help of one of the refugee women, and that's where you come in."

Al Leon took over, "The power shorted out when the incident occurred. Because The Machine wasn't shut down according to procedure, it's unstable, and it could go up."

"By go up," Cynthia interrupted, "you mean go kaboom."

"Yes, exactly. But the power can't be restored remotely. It can only be done from inside the facility."

"There's a master switch that needs to be thrown," Champagne added.

"Like in Jurassic Park?" Cynthia ventured.

"Like in Jurassic Park. Once that's done, everything

else can be reactivated; communications, wi-fi, everything. And that includes The Machine. We need you to make contact with the refugees, help one of them find their way to the master switch and then guide her through the process."

"Okay, but how do I do that if communications are down?"

"There is a way."

The Central Security control room in the top tier was incredible. Cynthia's first thought was that it was like something out of a James Bond movie. She then upgraded that assessment to the bridge of the *Starship Enterprise*. The room was bright, white and arranged in an amphitheatre style, with crescents of workstations all facing a wall of massive screens.

No, not the Enterprise, she decided. *NASA.*

The workstations weren't just desks with keyboards and screens on them, either. They were integrated control panels. Cynthia felt a surge of excitement at the thought of being one of the people who sits at a control panel doing important things that involves space travel.

Just wait till I tell my folks!

She'd been met off the plane by the Persons in Black, Al and Champagne, which had given rise a lot of cocked eyebrows and excited chatter among her colleagues. They had taken her straight down to the top tier to be photographed for her brand new and far flashier SmartCard. Also, she had been fingerprinted. Fingerprinted! Cynthia had never been fingerprinted in her life. She had toyed with questioning the privacy implications of having her fingerprints taken and kept on file, but she was enjoying the experience of feeling so goddam important just a little too much.

As she was led through the control room, flashy new SmartCard hanging from flashy new Agents of Shield lanyard (Cynthia hadn't been able to resist), her new colleagues had one by one looked up and given this new girl with the tattoos, blonde mohawk and horn-rimmed glasses a knowing nod. God, this felt good. For the first time in her life she had started to feel as if she may – just may – be on an upward trajectory.

My stock is rising, she'd thought. *I'll finally be able to get a turntable and start that vinyl collection I've been dreaming about.*

"There's a CCTV and loudspeaker system," Champagne explained, "and as its power source is above ground, it didn't short out. Any questions?"

"Yes. Why aren't there any seven-foot-tall blue women?"

"Yeah," said Al, somewhat shiftily, "that *is* a good question. Before I answer that, I would remind you about the non-disclosure agreement you signed earlier today when you officially accepted your new position."

"Okaaaay."

Al wheeled his office chair forward and took control of the console. After clicking through several files the screen opened up to a recorded CCTV view of the underground lab. On the screen was a row of pods, presumably the ones the test subjects had been lying in when whatever happened, happened. Then two scientists – Cynthia knew they were scientists because they were wearing lab coats and carrying tablet computers – wandered into shot.

"This was just before the incident," Champagne explained.

The two scientists talked between themselves for a few moments, and then a blue, hairless man, at least seven feet in height, wandered up to them. This blue man appeared to be wearing a nappy.

"Jesus," Cynthia gasped. "I don't know what I should be more disturbed by, the fact that he's blue or the fact he's wearing a nappy."

The blue guy appeared to be chatting amiably with the scientists and…laughing? Cynthia struggled to make sense of this, having previously seen two of these blue guys attempting to murder two women and a baby.

Another scientist accompanied by two more blue giants appeared onscreen. One of these blue giants was female. She was about a foot shorter than her male counterpart but also completely bald.

"Dude! She's topless!" Cynthia exclaimed.

Al clicked on another POV and the view widened.

"Now you can see all the pods," Al pointed out. "One for each of the twenty test subjects. Ten male, ten female."

"Couldn't they at least have given her a sports bra or something?"

"Please concentrate, Cynthia. This was the point where they were preparing to be put under."

"Put under?"

"Put into stasis," Champagne explained. "In order to survive a jump, the test subjects, the astronauts, would need to be in suspended animation. It takes one day to fully put them under and then ten to bring them back out. This was the final test. If this worked they'd be officially mission-ready."

"Define 'jump'," Cynthia said.

"Leaving space at one point and re-entering at another."

"No freaking way! So where were they supposed to be going?"

"That's classified."

"You're no fun."

All twenty of the test subjects were now in shot and, swarming around them, a small army of scientists and engineers. Cynthia noticed two of the engineers in their blue overalls attaching a large, white flexible tube to one of the pods.

"What're they doing?"

"It's through there that the supercooling agent is introduced," Champagne explained.

"Therapeutic hypothermia is already used in some more advanced hospitals," added Al. "Where a patient is cooled down slowly to reduce the heart rate and blood pressure. That formed the basis for what you're seeing now, but this is light years ahead of that. Literally."

"Basically, the body is supercooled quickly, freezing the vital organs and the brain when they're at peak ability," Champagne went on. "It's a process that would kill you or I, but the modifications made to the test subjects' bodies make it possible."

"Yes, but whereas the cooling is done quickly," Al continued, "the thawing has to be done slowly, in order for the brain functions to be maintained. So, the test subjects were supposed to be brought back up to thirty-seven degrees over a period of ten days, but when the incident occurred, this happened…"

Al clicked off the video clip and returned to the menu of files. Then he clicked on another one. The scene was much the same, but the lab was darker now. Despite the dim lighting, Cynthia could see, through the glass tops of the pods, the blue test subjects, serenely reposed and deep in sleep. There were a few scientists milling around, checking the readouts on the sides of the pods and making notes on their tablets. An engineer, a petite lady in a blue overall with red hair, wandered into shot and started chatting to one of the scientists.

"Okay," Al began. "At this point, the test subjects had been in their pods, in stasis, for one full day. All life signs were good, everything was just as it should be, but there was a massive power surge. We think it might have been caused by the hurricane, but we're still trying to confirm that. The lab should have been safe from any meteorological interference as it's underground. But anyway, as well as shorting out all the power in the lab,

146

the surge basically fried the test subjects' brains, leaving them with nothing but their most primary functions."

As Al was explaining this, the scene on the recording changed, and holy hell erupted.

An explosion, off camera, blew the scientists and the engineer off their feet. The lighting became intermittent. A hose detached and started spewing supercooling fluid, filling the lab with a dense, white fog. The engineer and the scientists in shot died instantly.

"Most of the technicians in the lab were killed by the supercooling fluid," Al explained. "Those that weren't were killed by the male test subjects a few hours later when they came round."

"And the female test subjects?" a slightly disturbed Cynthia asked.

"Raped and killed by the male ones," Al answered coldly.

"Show her," said Champagne.

"Look, if it's all the same to you…" Cynthia pleaded, her hands aloft in a gesture of surrender.

"Comes with the job."

Al guided the cursor to the 'forward' icon and the image accelerated. Not much happened, it seemed, for the next few minutes as Cynthia watched. However, those few minutes translated to over four hours in real time. Once the fog had completely cleared, several scientists and engineers appeared, zipping around the frame at superhuman speed. Al clicked a command and the picture returned to normal speed. The light continued to flicker.

"The technicians you can see had to wait until the lab had returned to a safe temperature before they could enter," said Champagne. "Watch what happens now…"

The scientists and engineers were rushing around the pods, checking the readouts, wiping away the sediment on the glass in order to peer in. The glass top of one of the pods suddenly exploded outwards, causing Cynthia to jump. The test subject had kicked it away.

At first, the giant blue man seemed confused. He all but fell out of the pod and was immediately besieged by technicians. They helped him to his feet and sat him down on the pod's edge. Cynthia watched as one of the scientists held up three fingers in front of his eyes. Another scientist shone a torch into them. The blue man swung a mighty arm and swatted her away. Then he grabbed the other scientist, the one who had been holding the fingers up, and pinned him against the wall, his long blue fingers wrapped around the smaller man's thin neck. This scientist's feet were about a metre off the ground.

An engineer rushed into shot and tried to pull the test subject away. He had his throat ripped out. Then another fibreglass top exploded outwards and a female test subject staggered out. The male test subject regarded her for a moment and then went for her, forcing her to the floor.

Then a third pod was kicked open. Then another. Then another.

"Not one of the site technicians survived, and the same goes for the female test subjects," Champagne solemnly explained. "The ones who weren't frozen to death were killed by the male test subjects; twenty technicians in all and ten female test subjects. It was a massacre."

"Oh my god," Cynthia murmured.

"Yes," Al said, nodding grimly. "SpaceWurd lost their entire LDST team in this incident, along with the test subjects. It's set their work back years."

"LDST?" Cynthia asked.

"Long distance space travel," Champagne confirmed.

"But that's not all," Al added.

"What? Wait? How could this possibly get any worse?" a dumbfounded Cynthia asked.

"The GSN have since recorded…"

"GSN?"

"Global Seismographic Network."

"What is it with you guys and acronyms? Jeez."

Al sighed and ploughed on. "The GSN has since recorded a significant increase in seismographic activity off the East Africa coast. We believe that The Machine is the cause of it. If it blows it'll take the entire island with it."

"Of course, that could also mean tsunamis big enough cause major loss of life in Madagascar. Mozambique and possibly Tanzania," Champagne added.

"And the fact the GSN is now picking up regular tremors means we're running out of time. We have to act now. Can we count on you, Cynthia?"

"Um…yes?" Cynthia replied with a bite of the lip.

"Good. Just one snag. Because of the time difference you'll have to stay late in order to complete this mission."

"Wait a minute. Did you just describe this as a mission?"

Champagne stepped forward. *Very* late," she stressed.

I can't believe I get to go on missions now, Cynthia thought with equal levels of excitement and panic. "Okay," she replied. And then, "Oh. That could be a problem, actually. I have to feed my cat."

"Is there someone who can do that for you?" Al asked.

Asking her Trump-supporting sister was out of the question. Cynthia hadn't spoken to her since November 2016, which just left her parents.

"Well, I suppose I could call my mom…"

"Excellent. Do that."

Cynthia sighed. *Well,* she thought, *I suppose this is how it is when you play with the big boys.*

***

The morning air was cool and refreshing, Buki was happy and content on his sun lounger and Esperance and

150

Godriva were enjoying a breakfast of Pop Tarts, peaches and coffee. From their rooftop vantage point, the sisters were looking out towards the ocean beyond the jungle. It was enshrouded in a mist that the sun had yet to burn away.

"How are you feeling today?" Esperance asked.

"Better today," Godriva answered. "I slept well."

"I know. There was another earthquake during the night and you did not stir."

"There was another quake?" Godriva asked. "How bad?"

"It was much like the first one. It didn't last long."

"I can't believe I slept through it."

"Neither can I."

"Did it wake Buki?"

"Yes. But he didn't cry. I cuddled him for a while and then he went back to sleep."

Godriva's throat was still raw from all the screaming during her breakdown of the previous day, but other than that she really was feeling better. She felt as though a malignant force had been exorcised from her. She felt cleansed.

"We *will* find a way off this island, you know," said Esperance.

"I know."

"Something will turn up. You'll see."

And at that, a new and mysterious voice echoed around the facility grounds.

"Hello! Can you hear me?"

Esperance and Godriva jumped, sending Pop Tarts flying.

"What was that?" Godriva yelped as she clung onto her sister.

"No idea!"

"Hello! Hello! I can see you on the CCTV camera. If you can hear me, please wave!"

Esperance and Godriva stared at each other with hope flashing in their eyes, both daring to believe that perhaps, just perhaps, salvation had finally come. They looked up at the CCTV camera, the one rising up from the roof. The one they had assumed was, like all the others, dead. Esperance gave a nervous wave.

And after a few seconds' pause: "Great!" This voice, despite booming through the loudspeaker system like a crack of doom, sounded friendly. "That's awesome! Say, can you speak English? Give me another wave if you can!"

This time, both Esperance and Godriva waved, their faces now blazing with promise and excitement.

"Cool! Okay, hi there! I'm Cynthia and I'm talking to you from Arizona in the US! Hope you're both okay there! And the baby too, obvs! She's a cutie! Or he! Anyway! We've only just got the CCTV and the speakers back online and we're working to get the other stuff up and running too! We're gonna come and get you off that island…"

The two sisters grabbed each other in celebration and screamed. However, it was premature.

"…but we need you to do something for us first! Have you guys been getting some, like, earthquakes by any chance?"

Esperance and Godriva responded with frantic nodding.

"Yeah. There's this big machine under the ground that's causing that, and it needs to be stabilised, and to do that we need you to reboot the power for the whole site, like in Jurassic Park! Then we'll be able to get you guys outta there! So, can you do that for me?"

Esperance gave a thumbs-up to the CCTV camera.

"Great stuff! So there's a master switch that needs to be thrown, but getting to it ain't gonna be easy! It means one of you has to go down to the underground lab and access the back-up control panel via the air conditioning vents! Okay? But I gotta warn ya, those big blue guys outside? Well, they came from the lab underground, and before they got out they killed everyone down there, so there's bodies everywhere. You gonna be able to handle that?"

Godriva gave Esperance a look. It said: 'over to you'. Her sister was a nurse, after all. She should be used to seeing dead bodies. Esperance gave another thumbs-up to the watching camera, but this one was far more cautious.

Back in the top tier control room, where it was pushing 10p.m., Cynthia, with a cup of coffee in hand, was sitting at a control panel watching the two young women on the other side of the world via her monitor.

She had instructions laid out on the desk in front of her and an earpiece-and-mic set clamped to her head, which flattened her mohawk. Positioned either side of her were Al Leon and Champagne Star. There were several other clandestine operatives scattered about in the control room, but none of them were dressed like the Men in Black. Only these two. So strange.

"Okay. Good. So here's what you need to do…" Cynthia said, knowing that seconds later her voice would be echoing all over the facility grounds far away on another continent.

***

Esperance made her way over to the giant H on the dusty ground, ignoring the howls and grunts from the few blue savages who were still gathered outside the fence. Raising an arm to block out the sun, she looked up to the roof of the living block where her sister was standing, holding Buki. Godriva waved Buki's little arm for him. Esperance waved back.

She opened up the hatch in the middle of the H where she and her sister had first emerged into the compound. Then, as instructed by this Cynthia girl from Arizona, she descended the ladder.

Godriva looked on as her sister disappeared into the ground and fought back a sob. She was afraid; afraid of what awaited her sister down there in the depths of this mysterious facility where something truly awful had already happened, and afraid she might never see her again.

Esperance would not let herself be deterred by whatever horrors awaited her where daylight could not penetrate. She was determined to let nothing stand between her and getting off this damn island once and for all.

Cynthia was already underground, of course, and far deeper than Esperance would be going. Despite the severity of the situation those two sisters over there in Africa were in, she was feeling good. She was glad to finally be able to do something to help. Via her monitor she saw that Esperance was now in the airlock, so she moved her mouse and clicked a command.

Esperance was standing in front of the airlock door, the one with the oval window that stood opposite the steel door. There was a hiss and it slid sideways. She felt a ghost of frigid air waft over her. In her hand was a torch. Cynthia had told her to bring one as the lights in the lab were faulty. Esperance aimed it into the darkness and switched it on.

Cynthia had warned her about what to expect – "It ain't gonna be pretty." – and she was right. What greeted Esperance's horrified eyes was carnage. A man in a lab coat was lying slumped against a table with his intestines in his lap. The expression on his face suggested he had been alive when he was gutted. An older woman, perhaps in her fifties, was lying on the floor, her body facing down, her face facing up. One of her arms was bent the wrong way, the other one was nowhere to be seen. A large man with a big beard, who Esperance recognised from the family photo in the bunkroom she had explored with her sister, was lying dead in the corner.

Cynthia with her big booming voice had said there were thirty bodies down here waiting to be found; twenty technicians and ten female test subjects. Given that these bodies had been lying untouched for the last four days, there was not much smell to speak of, for which Esperance was grateful. This was due to the underground cold. Esperance was wearing the blue boiler suit she had recovered from one of the bunk rooms. However, before coming down she had it tied it off at the waist and had just a thin vest on top. She shivered. Laying her torch on the ground, she slipped her arms into the boiler suit and zipped it up. She was ready now, ready to do this. She retrieved her torch and stepped inside.

She aimed her flashlight at the far-right corner of the room, just below the ceiling. There, as Cynthia had promised, was a grille. It was into this vent that she had to go. It looked big enough for her to fit into so that was one doubt about this plan that could be dismissed. However, she'd need something to stand on, and the only thing that could do the job was the table, the one that had the dead man with his guts hanging out slumped up against it. Without making the mistake of pausing to think, Esperance yanked the table away, leaving the

156

man's head to fall back and crack on the cold, hard floor. Esperance winced, but it made her remember an instruction given to her by Cynthia. Slowly, uneasily, she approached the dead man, removed the SmartCard and lanyard he had around his neck and hung it around her own. That done, she hopped up onto the table and wrapped her fingers around the grille. It came away easily and she placed it quietly on the table next to her feet. She had not wanted to throw it to the ground as she was wary about making too much noise. Cynthia had assured her she would be alone, but she couldn't help but wonder if…

Swallowing her anxieties, she pushed her torch into the vent and hauled herself in after it.

Here in this dark, confined space, Esperance's mind flashed back to her running in open country. That was always when she felt at her freest. Running helped to keep her mind clear as well as her body lithe and fit. Back home in Burundi, she would squeeze in a five-mile run every day Monday to Friday, then a longer run on a Saturday, perhaps fifteen miles. On Sunday she would rest. She was glad of her fitness regime now. It meant she was slim and agile enough to crawl through this shaft with relative ease. She also had the stamina to do it speedily and stealthily.

Let's just get this done, she thought. *In – do the job – and out again.*

The 'out again' part was, if all went to plan, going to be a lot easier. With the power restored all the interior doors would be back online, which meant Esperance could use her 'borrowed' SmartCard to open them and walk back out. Simple.

Up ahead was a junction. Cynthia had instructed her to turn right here and then keep going all the way to the end. Esperance did as she was told and saw a long square tunnel, around three feet high and wide, stretching off into the black distance. There was flickering light at intermittent points, flashing up through the floor, probably from the rooms below, and let in through the grilles. She didn't like the look of this. Not one bit. She had never been one to suffer from claustrophobia, but the prospect of crawling through this tight space for god knows how long would have got anyone sweating, especially considering all the freaky things that had happened so far.

Okay, just keep moving forward, she told herself. *Eyes on the prize.*

She held her breath and listened. All she could hear was the soft hum of electrical machinery from somewhere. After all, the lights were still flickering and the air con was still working, so it was to be expected. She steeled herself and started inching forward. Then her imagination began working against her. It threw at her images of hungry brown rats scuttling down the vent towards her. If something like that happened, would she be able to back-up quickly enough to escape? Of course not. She'd be trapped in there with them squealing, biting and gnawing at her.

Oh for goodness' sake, pull yourself together, she thought.

After the rats came the spiders. But not just any spiders. No, her imagination had something special in store. These were her most feared kind: the ogre-faced spider, a species that truly lived up to its name. Thousands of them, each with its two big, black forward-facing eyes, crawling over each other, scuttling towards her, swarming over the ceiling mere inches above her head and dropping down onto her, finding their way into her overalls. She couldn't help but shudder.

I thought you were supposed to be on my side, her inner voice said to her imagination.

No way, her imagination replied. *Suffer, bitch.*

There was no imagination necessary for her next scare. She reached the first grill, casting its flickering light up into the vent. She peered through it and into the room below. She could only see a small section of it, but it was obvious the room was vast. There was a female test subject in her eye line, lying face down – for which Esperance was grateful – in a pool of dried blood, now blackened. The woman was blue, tall, bald and naked. One of her arms was lying underneath her torso, twisted at an unnatural angle. There was a set of bloody footprints, remarkably large, leading away from her.

"Bless you," Esperance whispered, not wanting to pass the dead woman by without some sort of commemoration, however tiny.

She crawled on, hoping her imagination would leave her alone for the rest of this uncomfortable mission. She realised that the deeper into the vent she crawled, the colder the air became. She felt her arms prickle with goosebumps. The sensation reminded Esperance of those chilly nights back home in Burundi. Yes, she was still thinking of Burundi as home.

There was more flickering light up ahead, emerging from the floor. Another grill revealing another room, perhaps another corpse. She approached it tentatively, not wanting to find herself staring into the eyes of a dead person, perhaps missing limbs, perhaps gutted. She stretched her neck forward and peered into the light. The first thing she saw was a hand lying knuckle side down on the floor, fingers outstretched. Esperance flinched and drew back.

Just go on. Don't look down, her reasonable inner voice suggested.

It was good advice, but there was something very peculiar about that hand. For a start it was very small and kind of grey. That it would be grey was unsurprising. Its owner had been dead for several days, after all. But it was so small that Esperance could not help but wonder if it belonged to child, perhaps a girl.

Why would anyone bring a child into this place?

Esperance decided that if there was a dead child down there, she did not want to see it, and so she shut her eyes and started shuffling forward on her elbows.

But then her inner voice piped up again: *But if it is a*

child, her parents might be out there somewhere wondering what happened to her. They'd need to know.

The logic here was inarguable, and so Esperance opened her eyes and, in that moment, her world changed forever.

Below her, lying on its back on the floor and staring up at her, was an alien. Esperance felt every single atom in her being turn to ice as, conversely, hot blood surged and roared in her ears. There could be no doubt about what it was. Its grey body was small, like that of a child, but its head was huge and its eyes were large, almond-shaped and deathly black. It could not have looked more alien if it tried.

Esperance's breaths came in tiny, terrified puffs. Her eyes watered and her throat tightened. She tried to swallow but couldn't. It was an alien. Here. Now. And it was looking back at her.

Should I say something? Esperance asked herself.

She decided that no, she was not going to say anything. Instead, she was going to get the hell out of there before her senses abandoned her completely. The walls of her reality could not bear the weight of something this huge, this…this…cataclysmic. She suddenly realised how infinitesimally tiny she was when compared to the universe from which this…thing had come. She was barely even a speck. She was nothing.

The planet! Did this creature come from the planet that Esperance and Godriva had seen filling the sky the previous night? Were there more of them? Could they come and go as they pleased?

I'm losing it here. Got to go. Got to go.

Slowly, as silently as possible, Esperance began shuffling back down the vent, the way she had come, not daring to take her bulging, terrified eyes from the alien, not even for a second. When all she had beneath her was the cold, metallic surface of the vent shaft, she found that she could breathe again. With her breaths came the urge to vomit – her stomach was churning – but she kept it down.

Gotta stay in control, she told herself. *Gotta stay in control.*

Nothing she had seen so far on this deranged island had prepared her for this. The blue savages? At least they were mostly human. But this? An actual alien? It was too much.

Come on, Esperance. Keep it together.

She closed her eyes, breathed in slowly and deeply and then exhaled. She repeated this over and over until she could physically feel her heart rate slowing. An empty space formed in her frantic mind, allowing her to think.

What do I do? How do I explain this to Godriva? How can we possibly stay here now? We have to get out. We need a plan. No! I know what I have to do. I have to reboot the power so we can get off this damn island, so they can come and rescue us. Which means I have to cross the grill and see...it...again.

Esperance did not relish the idea of that and every

instinct in her mind and body was screaming at her to get the hell out of there. But beneath the cacophony of terror, her rational voice continued speaking, determined to be heard.

The alien is dead. It didn't move. It just lay there staring up. It didn't react when it saw me. It's dead, like everything else down here. Dead.

Esperance decided that if the alien was indeed dead, she may – just may – be able to deal with this, to keep her head and complete her mission.

I can do this, she thought. *Don't wait. Don't think. Just do.*

She forced her body forward, shuffling on her elbows. The sheer willpower involved was titanic. Then she was over the grill, over *it*. It was still there, lying motionless, staring blankly up. Esperance felt in control. She was handling this.

I'm going to be okay, she decided.

She had enough control now to study the room the creature was lying in. It was pretty bare. There was a simple chair, nothing fancy. There was also a desk, but nothing on it; no PC or paper or pens. There was something to lie on which looked like those tables that the physiotherapists used back at the hospital. But most interestingly of all, there was a clear fibreglass wall.

Is this a cell? Esperance wondered. *Was the alien a prisoner?*

She looked back to it again, the motionless alien, and wondered what had happened to it. How had it died? All the scientists and engineers had perished at the hands of the blue test subjects, but not this. There was no sign of any bodily trauma.

And then it blinked.

Esperance felt her muscles harden. It blinked again, several times, rapidly, as if coming back from a deep sleep, and then it began to stand up. Mad with terror, all Esperance could do was stare. She tried to move but her joints had fused. The creature was standing upright now and looking straight into Esperance's eyes, regarding her, studying her. Then came the final horror. Smoothly, effortlessly, it stepped up onto the chair and then onto the desk and reached up, extending its long, alien fingers towards her. And that's when Esperance started screaming.

It took a few seconds for the screams to find their way through the ventilation system and reach the bunkroom where Godriva was breastfeeding Buki. They were feint, but that did nothing to lessen the fearsome terror they carried; Esperance's terror, her sister's terror. This terror then became Godriva's too.

"Sister," was all she could whisper.

Esperance, screaming beyond limit, moved. As she flailed and thrashed and reversed her way back down the shaft towards the hatch she saw four long, grey, bony fingers and a thumb wrap around the grill and start shaking it, sending abrasive, metallic clangs clattering through the vent. The clanging and the screaming mixed together in the miles of vents and ducts to become a hellish cacophony. When this sound also found its way to the bunkroom, Godriva picked up Buki and fled.

Esperance's imagination kicked into overdrive, assaulting her with images of the alien crawling through the shaft towards her, reaching her, wrapping its inhuman fingers around her, screaming in her face with a voice that was not human. But the grille was holding, for now. This one, being horizontal, was screwed in. It seemed to take Esperance forever to reach the junction, but when she did she remembered she needed to turn left. Now that the dreadful alien fingers were out of her sightline she could focus again. She felt the presence of her sister and her nephew somewhere above, like homing beacons, calling to her, guiding her back.

Then her feet found the hole in the wall and she slithered through it, dropping onto the table. She jumped down onto the floor and sprinted past the bodies which this time she hardly even noticed. She flew up the ladder and emerged into the blinding sunlight. Slamming the hatch shut, she ran for the living block, dust flying up at her heels. But before she could even reach the door, a panic-stricken Godriva, with Buki in arms, came tumbling out through it.

"Sister? What is it? What happened?"

But Esperance could not speak. She did not have the words to describe what she had seen or what had happened. All she could do was gasp for air. Godriva came to her, and on their knees in the dirt they held each other and cried. Meanwhile, beyond the stainless-steel

165

fence, the giant blue savages paced and growled.

***

Through electronic eyes half a world away, Cynthia looked on as the refugee woman exploded out of the hatch. The images had no sound. Cynthia was also silent. Then the other woman, the one with the baby, ran into shot. Much crying and hugging ensued. Cynthia looked over her shoulder to see Champagne Star jotting something down in a notepad.

After a few moments, the two women got up from the dusty ground and made their way inside the living block. The woman with the baby seemed to be supporting the one who had been underground. She looked as though she were about to faint.

"Go to the roof," Al Leon said. "Just in case."

Cynthia clicked on the POV from the camera on the roof. It showed the seating area with the sun loungers and umbrellas out. In the background she could see the high, stainless-steel fence and the expanse of plain beyond. Scattered across the plain were three or four of the giant blue test subjects. Cynthia shivered. And then the two women and the baby appeared.

Again, Champagne Star made a note.

The woman who had ventured down into the lab looked like she was in a state of shock, her face desperate and tear-streaked. Cynthia noticed that she had a sheet of paper and a marker pen in her hand. She

166

looked angrily into the camera and then squatted down on the floor. She was writing or drawing something. The other woman, who was still holding her baby, kept looking to her sister, into the camera and then back again.

"What's happened?" Cynthia murmured. "What's she doing?"

Finally, the distraught young woman stood up and held the piece of paper up to the camera. It had on it a simple line drawing of a face. The face had a small, pointed chin, a very large cranium, a tiny nose and mouth and huge eyes which were scribbled in black. Beneath the drawing was a single word in big black letters: ALIEN.

Cynthia stared at the image in silence. *What do I say to her?* she thought. Eventually, she looked over her shoulder to find that her two minders had been replaced by her new supervisor, Elise Diamond.

"Miss Dowley? You're relieved. You can go home."

"But it's the middle of the night," Cynthia complained. "The plane doesn't leave for, like, another six hours or something. And I'm back on duty at eight anyway."

"Not any more you're not. Take the day off and come back the day after."

Elise was not someone you ever wanted to mess with. She was hard-faced, volatile and subsisted on a diet of painkillers, Red Bull, chocolate and wine. And possibly cocaine too, according to the rumours.

Sulkily, Cynthia sloped off to the elevator and began to wonder if this promotion was really worth the extra money. A piece of advice courtesy of her father drifted into her fatigued mind: "Never give up on a new job in the first week. When you start a new one, you always get 'first week blues'. Always. It's because you have no idea what's going on and it gets you down, and you think, 'Gee, why did I take this stupid job? Why didn't I just stay where I was, with my friends, where I knew what I was doing?' But after a week things always look brighter. You get to know a few people, you get your head around how things work. So never give in to the 'first week blues'."

"First week blues," Cynthia mumbled to herself as she emerged from the elevator into the muted glass-and-steel reception area. Outside, the black curtain of the night sky was pricked with stars. There was no sign of the security guy who would normally be on the desk. Must have gone to take a leak, or something. Cynthia shrugged. She considered for a moment calling Alison and asking if she'd come and pick her up in her car. But how could she do that? It was around two in the morning!

Seeing no other option, Cynthia laid herself down on a row of cushioned seats in the waiting area, placed her specs on her chest and closed her eyes. In her mind's eye she saw the drawing that the woman on the other side of the world had held up to the camera.

Alien, she thought as she drifted away.

Chapter 14

After showing the girl in Arizona the drawing of the alien via the CCTV camera, a distraught Esperance had insisted that she, Godriva and Buki all return to the (relative) safety of the bunkroom and lock the door. She had been in a near-hysterical state when she'd emerged from the hatch, crying and nonsensical. Godriva had never seen her big sister in such extreme distress and it had chilled her to the marrow of her bones.

She had insisted on making her trembling and blubbering sister a cup of tea to try and calm her nerves. It was a small gesture, but Godriva wanted to do something for her. Just something. It seemed to help, because Esperance was now talking rationally again, even though she was still twitchy and shaking.

"There are things going on here, in this facility, that we can't imagine. Not just the blue men and the alien. All the people who worked here were ripped apart, just like the ones we came ashore with. It was carnage. And the facility beneath us is like nothing I've ever seen before. I saw the pods where the blue men were made."

"God," was all Godriva could say as she held her son close. Her face was scrunched up in concentration. "And you're absolutely sure that the…the alien, or whatever it is, was locked up?"

"It was definitely an alien, and yes. It was in a cell. It had a clear wall right across so there was no way it could get out."

Hopefully, Esperance added in her mind.

She continued: "And there was just a chair and a desk and something to lie on, just like a cell. God, you should have seen the way it looked at me. And when it stood on the desk and reached out for me…"

Godriva nodded without really understanding.

"We've stumbled into something here," Esperance went on, "something that was not meant to be found. That's why no one's come to rescue us. And now they want me to reboot this machine of theirs and I can't stop wondering why? What happens when I do?"

"To stop the earthquakes," said Godriva. "So that we can leave…"

"But what happens if it's not just the machine? What if I reboot that and the whole site comes back online? Will the cell door holding the alien open?"

Godriva thought about that for a moment. "That's a good question, sister."

***

Cynthia was afraid, and she had good reason to be.

170

Instead of heading straight home after finally getting out of the spaceport, she decided to call into a familiar Old Town diner to mull things over.

She had seen too much, heard too much and now, she was pretty sure, knew too much. There was just one thought rattling around her brain and it wasn't a particularly pleasant one: *They're gonna bump me off! They're gonna bump me off!*

But hey, come on Cynth, she reassured herself, *this is the real world here. Corporations don't really go bumping off their employees because they happened to be gazing at the wrong monitor at the wrong time, do they? Hell no, because bumping off employees means getting other employees to do the bumping, which means yet more people knowing stuff they're not supposed to know, which means that the original bumpers then have to be bumped off too. I think this is what's known as an infinite regression.*

And yet, this logical conclusion was doing nothing to calm her jittery nerves as she sat in the corner of the quiet diner, devouring a bagel and a much-needed coffee.

Jesus, how happy she'd been when she landed this SpaceWurd job just a few short years ago. Oh sure, it was only a Remote Security Monitor and it was pretty dull. She'd watch CCTV footage, file the occasional report, make sure everything was as it should be. Now and again she'd have to open a door, or even close one if things got really exciting. And yes, the hours sucked as it involved shift-work, but the pay was very good for what it was. But best of all was she got to come into work every day with a clean slate. She didn't have an in-tray with tasks piling up in it, she didn't have deadlines, she didn't have to worry about preparing presentations or writing projections or hitting targets. In other words, all the soul-blackening crap that most other people had to endure day after day after day after day, she was spared.

And dude, she was working for SpaceWurd! The company founded by that billionaire guy Byron Wurd whose dream it was to make space travel an everyday part of our lives. The billionaire who wanted to have spaceships flying between Earth and the Moon and Mars and beyond. Sure, it all sounded a bit crazy when said out loud, but when *he* said it, when Mr B said it, it all sounded like it might actually happen. And here was Cynthia, riding along on this interstellar wave. And okay, in the underground Arizona monitoring room she never even got to see the light of day, let alone outer space, but she was working for SpaceWurd!

So yeah, her job was pretty cool.

However...

The freaky shit that had kicked off a few days previously had started to get really *really* freaky. Actually, it had passed way beyond freaky and was now deep into the realm of the downright terrifying. She had seen things she could never unsee, like scientists being beaten to death by giant blue savages, for example, and the look on that young woman's face when she'd held up the alien drawing.

Christ, had that girl *really* seen an alien? Was there actually an extra-terrestrial in the lab facility? Cynthia tried to get her head around how it could possibly be so. Surely someone would have blabbed by now if there was. Alison's monologue about misinformation crashed back into her head. So yeah, even if someone did blab, there'd be so much crazy shit surrounding that particular nugget of info that no one would believe it anyway, except maybe the conspiracy theory crazies who believed anything as long as was on the internet and not in a newspaper. *They'd* believe it, but that mere fact meant that every right-thinking (i.e. sane) citizen wouldn't. So, Catch 22.

Cynthia had not yet had the chance to take advantage of her top tier status and explore the lab facility fully via CCTV. If there was an alien in there, surely there'd be a camera on it. There was a camera on everything else, after all.

She was questioning everything now. How could she not? No one had ever given her the full picture of what was going on at that facility. Sure, that Neal Terry dude had told her and her colleagues that the 'test subjects' were being prepped for long-distance space travel, but she was no longer convinced that we were talking about Mars here. In the one (admittedly long) day she'd spent in the Central Security control room, she'd heard brainiacs talking about 'light year event horizons' and 'superstring theory' and 'light leaps' and 'wormholes'. These test subjects, these astronauts who had now all lost their minds, were being readied for something beyond incredible, she was convinced of it. They were being sent to the farthest reaches of the universe.

Are we as a species really at that point? she wondered. *Is the cosmos about to be opened up to us? Are we about to enter a new phase in human history? But where were the test subjects being sent to? And for what purpose? Were they explorers? Were they envoys to an alien world, to the world of the alien in the facility? Is the alien itself an ambassador?*

No clue there, but something else popped into her mind. Al Leon and Champagne Star had told her about 'The Machine', but had made a point of not spelling out what it did exactly. Cynthia had popped the question, but lips had remained frustratingly sealed.

Cynthia had also heard various scientists talking about it, but always in the most opaque terms. Obviously, none of it was opaque to them because they were all geniuses, but to the average man or woman in the street: opaque.

So, it was 'The Machine' this and 'The Machine' that, and Cynthia had become convinced that this 'Machine', the one that was so impressive it came with its very own 'The', was the thing that was going to be sending these giant blue 'test subjects' hurtling across the void to god knows where.

She looked around at the handful of other breakfast

patrons in the diner. There was the pretty Muslim girl in the white headscarf who seemed to be sitting in the same place every time Cynthia visited, tapping away at her laptop with a pile of books next to her. Cynthia always assumed she was studying for something. Then there was the crazy Christian dude with the tattoos who dressed like a rock star and was often to be seen ranting at passer-by outside Starbucks (from where he'd been banned) on North Scottsdale Road. Cynthia hoped these two wouldn't notice each other. The last thing she needed right now was a theological showdown. She already had quite enough on her mind.

She finished up her bagel and coffee – brewed in-house, no less – and packed up her laptop, which went everywhere with her in her shoulder bag.

Better go home and feed Mashed Potato, she decided as she stepped out into the hushed and chilly morning. She headed for East India School Road to catch a bus, looking back over her shoulder now and again to make sure she wasn't being followed. Then she remembered seeing an episode of The Wire where McNulty's kids were doing 'front n follow', so she checked if there was anyone keeping tabs on her from the front too. There wasn't, or at least there didn't seem to be. In fact, there was no one near her in any direction, but that didn't necessarily mean that they weren't watching. They might be up on a rooftop. They might be…

She chastised herself. *Oh, for fuck's sake, Cynthia! You're being ridiculous!* But then, given all she had seen over the last few days, was she really?

Of all the conspiracy theories out there, the UFO one had always been her fave. When it was just herself and Mashed Potato in her apartment at night and she was flicking channels, she could never pass over 'Ancient Aliens' or 'UFOs Caught on Tape' or 'Area 51 – The Truth'. She supposed she enjoyed the whole UFO thing more than any other because she actually *wanted* it to be true. What a crazy and exciting world it would be if there really were flying saucers in the skies above and aliens abducting people and shit. And besides, who really wants to be alone in the universe? That's a scary thought right there, far scarier than *not* being alone!

So she and Mashed Potato had watched video footage that purported to show the alien bodies recovered from Roswell in 1947. She had seen three pill-shaped UFOs flying over the surface of the moon which had been filmed by an astronomer through a telescope here on Earth. She had seen an ISS astronaut putting his hand over the camera when a mysterious light had flown into view behind him. And she had seen a photo of a UFO through the window of which you could actually make out two occupants. Crazy.

But none of that had chilled her the way that young woman's drawing of an alien face had.

***

Godriva had taken it pretty well, all things considered.

At first, she seemed to struggle to comprehend what her sister was telling her, but Esperance slowly realised that it was not a question of understanding or denial, it was a question of imagination.

But of course Godriva had believed her sister. Why wouldn't she? Just look at all the crazy things that had already happened since washing up on this damn island! But this? An alien? Here? In this facility? Right now? It was a concept too huge for Godriva's mind to successfully grapple with. It was too 'out there' to be contextualised. There was no handy technical manual for dealing with it. It was something that needed to be seen first-hand so that the gravity of it could be absorbed.

Godriva had stared hard into Esperance's eyes and had seen truth in them, but she'd betrayed no reaction. There'd been no freak out, no tears, no insisting that they get the hell out of there right now. She had just swallowed it, and this had Esperance worried.

She was concerned that her sister might be freaking out inside, which was never healthy. Godriva was already on a knife-edge following the death of the boy, and now she'd just had another weight dumped on her slender shoulders. And this one was a big one. But in truth, Godriva had chosen to deal with it quietly and in her own way, which involved locking it away somewhere inside her mind, leaving her free to carry on breathing, carry on eating and carry on looking after her baby. In other words, to carry on surviving.

After all, what else could they do?

"What do you think it did?" Godriva asked.

"What do you mean?"

"What do you think it did? The alien. You know, to get locked up?"

Esperance looked at her sister as if she'd grown a second head.

"Well, I don't know. Shoplifting?"

"I only asked," Godriva grumbled.

"It's an alien! For all we know it might have wanted to take over the world!"

Buki could sense the dark clouds of disharmony gathering so he started jabbering, desperate to bring his mother's attention back to himself. Godriva picked him up and rocked him gently.

"So what are we going to do now?" she asked. "I mean, we can't stay here, can we?"

"No, but we can't leave either. The second we set foot outside we'll be set upon by those giant blue men. We have no choice but to stay. At the least the alien is locked up."

"Like us, you mean."

"Yes. Like us."

"But what about getting the power back on and stabilising this machine of theirs?"

"I don't know," Esperance said forlornly. "But what I *do* want to know is, why didn't the girl in Arizona tell us about the alien?"

Usually, Cynthia would arrive home from work itchin' to get Twitchin', but not today. Having just spent a fraught night grappling with intermittent sleep in the foyer of the SpaceWurd spaceport, she was desperate for some quality shut-eye. She kicked off her shoes, removed her glasses, crashed out on her (unmade) bed and invited Mashed Potato to join her, which he did.

If anyone had looked through Cynthia's bedroom window at this point, they'd have seen a young woman deep in blissful sleep with a big ginger cat curled up next to her, purring happily. However, the serenity of the scene would have belied the feverish thoughts that were festering within Cynthia's exhausted, labyrinthine mind.

I'm lying here on my bed. That's my reality. But there's a being out there who's piloting a spaceship over the surface of the moon, and that's his reality. Or hers. Or its. And the only thing keeping me and it apart is this ridiculous veil we've constructed, made of jobs and debt and reality TV and nice furnishings. But there are beings out there who have spaceships and can travel astronomical distances instantaneously, and if they break down they can fix them cos that's what they do, and they're flying over the surface of the moon which is so fucking close to us that it doesn't even matter. They're aliens, and they're here!

While Cynthia had been eating her bagel and sipping

a coffee in the Old Town diner, she had been reading up on all the crazy conspiracy theories she could find concerning the SpaceWurd company. Only now most of them didn't seem all that crazy. She felt as though she was drowning in a sea of half-truths, misinformation, elaborations, exaggerations and outright lies. Oh, and the occasional grain of truth. The trouble was, how does one pick out the grain of truth from the chaff? As a member of the 'top tier' she was now 'on the inside'. She had peeked behind the curtain and what she'd seen there had knocked her sensibilities sideways.

This company was developing technology that was way ahead of the curve. Tech that up until now Cynthia thought only existed in Marvel Comics. The scientists at that East Africa lab had been talking about sending people to a rendezvous in another galaxy. Well, not just talking about it, but actually working on it! Those people, the 'test subjects', were being 'adapted' or 'enhanced' in order to survive the trip. They were going to be travelling 'pan-dimensionally', leaving reality here and re-entering it there.

And on the flip side of the coin was what the company was telling the public. None of this was making it to the mainstream news outlets. Oh no. According to the press releases, SpaceWurd was in the 'early stages' of developing a 'viable NASA alternative' for the 'future of commercial space travel in America', or something.

So now, as a SpaceWurd pawn, or doormat, or

however she wanted to consider herself, Cynthia had become a tiny part of the misinformation factory, just as her on/off girlfriend Alison had surmised. Al had been bang on the money, Cynthia had to admit. Cover-ups were for mugs. They never lasted. Word always got out somehow, even if it was spilled from somebody's deathbed. So whenever some titbit of info or a piece of video did make it out there into the public sphere, the bullshit factory would simply crank into gear and start burying it. A genuine sighting could be swarmed by a bunch of somewhat less compelling sightings, easily debunked. A genuine piece of video footage would find itself besieged by questions about the veracity of the person who had uploaded it. And before you knew it lots of other, somewhat less convincing bits of film had mysteriously emerged under the same name, thus debunking the genuine footage. God, it was so simple it was brilliant!

And as Cynthia continued to plummet into this dark abyss of misinformation and bullshit, the hitherto glorious albeit innocent conversations she had once enjoyed with her friends suddenly struck her as being monumentally inconsequential.

"Say, have you heard the new Sheer Mag album? Fucking ace!"

Yeah, it is. But even though I love Sheer Mag cos they have that great logo, that killer guitar player who oozes cool without even trying and a fantastic lead singer who sometimes sounds like a young Michael Jackson despite being a woman who's maybe in her late twenties, I can't just pretend that there aren't aliens flying spaceships around the moon. And maybe because of what I've seen they have to make me disappear, so that's what's going to happen. One night (or day, as I work shifts) I'll suddenly find myself paralysed, and then I'll become aware that there's something in the room with me, and I'll move my eyes because I can't move anything else and I'll see one of them standing next to me in the dark; an alien, a 'grey', with its small body, large head and huge almond-shaped eyes. And it'll put a finger to my head and I'll blank out and later come to on its spaceship and...and...

There was a knock at the door.

Cynthia's consciousness was dragged back into her body, which felt about four times its usual weight. Had she actually managed to fall asleep there? Amazing, really, given the kind of day (or rather, night) she'd had. Funny, she could have sworn someone just knocked on her door.

Another knock.

Mashed Potato was on full alert now, and he wasn't the only one.

"It's okay, boy," Cynthia said. "It's probably nothing."

She didn't believe that, however. No one ever came calling for her unannounced. No one. Ever. She stealthily tiptoed through her tiny living room and into the kitchen, where the door was situated.

"Who is it?" she timidly asked.

It was a woman's voice who answered. "Champagne Star and Al Leon."

Cynthia's heart almost erupted. "What do you want?"

Champagne's reply came through the wood sounding friendly, reassuring. "Cynthia, I know you must be very worried, but Al and I have been reassigned, we're leaving, but we wanted to talk to you before we go. We feel there are things you ought to know."

Cynthia had no reason to trust her but, Jesus Christ, she wanted to. She really did. Trusting someone was so much easier than fearing them. She opened the door on the chain and peered through. Sure enough, there was Champagne Star and there was Al Leon, both in their civvies, each with a suitcase next to them.

"You haven't got anyone with you, have you?" Cynthia enquired through narrowed eyes.

Champagne Star opened her arms and spread her hands, as if demonstrating she was unarmed. "It's just us, Cynthia. Honestly."

They really didn't look like they were about to kidnap or even kill her, but maybe that's what they wanted Cynthia to think. Nevertheless, Cynthia was tired and confused and did not have the energy to be combative, so she opened the door and instantly regretted it.

Champagne and Al didn't have normal eyes, they had agents' eyes. Cynthia watched as they darted around, taking in every detail of her slovenly domicile before filing what they'd seen away for future use. And in that moment, Cynthia saw herself through those agents' eyes, and oh my fucking days she did not like what she saw. Not one bit.

There were the posters on the wall; Butcher Babies, L7, Joan Jett, Sheer Mag, Megadeth, Stitched Up Heart. Strewn over the back of the sofa were the Sumo Cyco socks, given to Cynthia by vocalist Sever after a gig, in honour of 'your awesome mohawk'. There was the Ibinez bass guitar, unplayed since the purchase of the PlayStation. There was the fruit bowl full of M&Ms. There were the knickers on the radiator. There was the pile of Bitch Planet comic books. There were the Pop Vinyls on the shelf.

These guys have probably killed people, Cynthia thought. *And I'm still buying toys.*

"My first ever gig was Joan Jett," Champagne said, nodding towards the image of Joan in her iconic pink jacket. "Nineteen ninety-four at the Huntridge in Vegas. I'll never forget it. Joan is the real thing. You can't fake what she has."

"I know, right?" said Cynthia with a cautious smile. "Joan rules."

Hey, maybe these guys aren't so bad after all, she thought. But then she stopped herself. *But what if they want me to think that?*

"Hello. Who's this?" asked Al as Mashed Potato sidled into the lounge to investigate.

"Oh. This is Mashed Potato. My cat."

Why did I say 'my cat'? Cynthia thought, squirming inside. *What? It didn't seem obvious enough?*

One short minute later and Champagne, now seated, had Mashed Potato purring and curling around her legs.

"Well," Cynthia said, "I suppose if Mashed Potato trusts you, I should too."

"No better judges of character than cats," Champagne said with a smile. "Got two at home, brothers, Freddy and Jason."

"I take it you're a horror fan then?"

"Big time."

"I kinda feel like I woke up in a horror movie this week," Cynthia said with a look in her eyes that indicated she was not entirely happy about this. She turned to Al, "So, you ready to tell me what book you were reading now? At the airport?"

"Sure. It was Tietam Brown by Mick Foley."

"Not familiar."

"He's a wrestler. It's kind of a passion of mine."

"Reading or wrestling?"

"Take your pick."

Cynthia eyed him up and down. He was clad in the casual attire she'd first seen him in at the airport; check shirt and jeans.

"Really? Didn't have you marked as the wrestler type."

"Oh, you see all types ringside, believe me."

"So, I have to ask," Cynthia said, addressing them

both. "Are those your real names?"

Champagne and Al shared a knowing smile.

"No, of course not," Champagne Star conceded.

"We're forbidden from disclosing our real names when on assignment," said Al.

"So what's really going down at the East Africa lab?"

"Even we don't know the full story," said Champagne as she fussed over Mashed Potato. "No one ever does in these scenarios."

"Plausible deniability," said Cynthia.

"Exactly."

"I watch a lot of TV."

"If no one has all the facts," Al added, "no one can reveal all the facts. Hence, you'll get fragments of information that seep out here and there over the years, and they'll be so polluted by misinformation that no one will ever be able to put all the pieces of the jigsaw together."

"It's like Chinese whispers," Champagne said. "If a UFO crashes and is witnessed, by the time that story has passed through ten people, it's become: a UFO crashed, alien bodies were recovered, one of them was still alive, feds swooped on the nearby town telling people what they saw and what they didn't, there were men in black…"

"In other words, you guys."

"Yes. It's all part of the great misinformation campaign, and boy does it work. Just ask Vladimir Putin. He used it to put you-know-who in the White

House."

"Tell me something I don't know. So have you guys actually recovered crashed UFOs?"

"If UFOs have been recovered," Al said, "we certainly weren't privy to it."

"I notice you didn't say no."

"She's a sharp cookie, this one," Champagne said to her colleague with a smile.

"To start at the beginning, are you guys really CIA?"

"We're not at liberty to say," said Al.

"Right. Gotcha. And what about those other guys who've been hanging around in the top tier?"

"Some of them are, and some are Air Force. Some from National Security."

"They keep secrets even from us," Champagne added.

"So how do I know this conversation isn't part of this great misinformation campaign?"

"We come in peace," Champagne said as she spread out the fingers of her right hand, Spock-style.

It was at this point that Cynthia thought: *Dang, she looks hot in that suit!*

Then Champagne dropped her bombshell. "Actually, we think you're being set up."

"Exsqueeze me?"

"We think you're being set up to take the fall for the inevitable moment when the shit hits the fan about what happened at the lab facility."

Al fixed her with a hard stare. "Something went very

wrong there, tragically. We all know that. But what we don't know is the true purpose of their machine."

"Long distance space travel. The blue guys were astronauts who were being prepped for…"

"Yes, that we *do* know, but there was something else going on, something underneath it all. Something to do with…"

"With the alien!"

Champagne raised her hands as if she were trying to calm down an aggressive assailant. "Now, we don't know what that young lady on the CCTV saw, but we've had no intel to suggest that…"

"Did you see the look on her face?" Cynthia blurted out. "She was scared out of her mind. She saw something alright!"

"That we don't doubt. But until we see something like that with our own eyes, we have to be sceptical."

"That's just the nature of the job," Al added, "and it's taught us not to jump to any conclusions without hard evidence."

"So do you have any hard evidence that I'm being set up?" Cynthia asked.

"No," Champagne replied, "but there's a pattern here we recognise. You weren't chasing promotion, were you?"

"No."

"And yet, here you are. So why do you think you were promoted?"

"Well, you guys promoted me. You tell me."

"No. The company promoted you. We just passed on the message."

"Ah. That Neal Terry guy said it's because I let those two women and the baby into the facility, so…"

Al interrupted, "Here's what's going to happen: whatever has gone down at that lab, or whatever is *going* to go down at that lab, they're going to pin it on you because you ignored protocol and let two 'terrorists' into the site."

Fox emphasised the word 'terrorists' by making speech marks with his fingers.

"But they're not terrorists."

"Of course they're not," Champagne said. "But that's how they'll be painted when the situation explodes."

"Okay. But why promote me?"

"You've heard the phrase keep your friends close and your enemies closer, I assume."

"Sure."

"It just wouldn't wash to try and pin the blame on – no offence – some random lowly employee. Then you'd have people asking serious questions about the facility's security."

"But if you're of a higher rank, as you are now," Al continued, "then that's different. They can pin it all on you."

"Oh, fuck," said Cynthia.

"Now, don't panic," Champagne said with a reassuring smile. "There are ways to defend yourself, number one being to start gathering evidence in your defence right now. Make copies of everything; such as your new contract, your NDA, relevant emails, even the fire safety sheet I'm assuming you have to sign every time you enter and leave the building."

"Yeah."

"And start keeping a diary," Al added. "Make a note of all incidents and at what time they occur, and whether or not you were in any way involved with them."

"You can beat this," Champagne said. "Don't be their patsy. If they try to pin anything on you don't be afraid to get mad. Raise your voice and tell them loudly and confidently that you have all this material evidence in your possession and if they try anything funny you'll march straight to the nearest TV station and give them everything you've got."

Al: "Once they realise you're not going to play the role of timid little employee out of her depth, they'll back off. They're afraid of troublemakers, and don't ever forget that."

"Yeah," said Champagne. "Never be afraid to be a troublemaker."

"Oh, don't worry," said Cynthia with a wink. "That's my speciality."

Al looked at his watch. "Okay, we have to hustle. We're due back in Langley and our flight leaves in one hour."

Langley! CIA! Cynthia thought. "One more thing," she said as her guests were standing up, ready to leave. "Why would you tell me any of this? Aren't you betraying orders or something by letting me in on it?"

"Our loyalties lie with our country, not with SpaceWurd," Champagne stated, and Cynthia could tell by the look in her eye that she really meant it.

The party said their goodbyes, and as Champagne, or whatever her real name was, walked off down the corridor, Cynthia found that she couldn't take her eyes off her.

In another life, perhaps.

Cynthia put some more food down for a grateful Mashed Potato and fixed herself a coffee. Then she dumped her ass down onto her beaten couch and pulled her laptop out of its bag. She logged on and accessed Scottsdale Airport's website. There were no flights scheduled for Norfolk International for the rest of that day. She tried Dulles. Still nothing. So were they bullshitting her about flying out to Langley? Did they just want her to think they were CIA? Maybe they were flying out from somewhere else, but if they were that didn't give them enough time to…

Cynthia caught herself. She was making herself paranoid again. It occurred to her then that paranoia was like a cancer. Left unchecked it would continue to grow and fester until it completely devoured you. Regardless of their flight arrangements, it was good advice they had given her. Yeah, she could get through this if she could just…

Her cell rang and she jumped.

Cynthia had the coolest ringtone in Arizona. It was

the bass intro to Megadeth's Peace Sells. If its intention was to make your spine prickle in anticipation of what was to come, then it was mission fucking accomplished. She scooped the phone up and checked the screen. It was Alison.

"Hey, Al."

"Hi, Cynthia. What are you up to? Don't tell me. Let me guess. You're playing computer games?"

"No. Not today."

"Cynthia? Are you okay? You don't sound yourself. Are you ill?"

"No. Just a bad night. I'm fine. Honest."

Cynthia wasn't fine, of course. Far from it.

"Cynth…"

Uh oh. Alison never addressed Cynthia as 'Cynth' unless there was bad news.

"…I was hoping to tell you this yesterday at the Rockingbird, but I didn't want to do it with Heather there."

Cynthia's brow furrowed into a concerned scowl. "Okaaaay."

"So I apologise for having to do this over the phone. It was not my intention."

"Okaaaay."

"But I'd rather you heard it from me as opposed to…"

"Okay. I get the picture. What's going on?"

"Audrey and I are seeing each other."

And with those seven words, the little piece of

Cynthia's world that was still solid turned to mist.

"WHAT? Audrey? But she's the biggest drama queen in Arizona!"

"I know she can be a little melodramatic…"

"Melodramatic? She'd give a sedative heartburn! Dude, I quit smoking for you! How could you…?"

"Cynthia. Please don't address me as 'dude'."

Cynthia felt her tear ducts begin to twitch. "Al. Please don't do this. Not now. I need you. You know I need you."

"Oh, Cynthia. When I broke it off this time you barely seemed to notice."

This much at least was true. When Alison had told her she wanted to break up Cynthia had all but shrugged. But this was because they had broken up countless times before and always ended up getting back together, so Cynthia naturally assumed it would be the same story again.

"I just didn't realise you actually meant it this time. Please give me one more chance. I can change. You know I can."

"Cynthia, this isn't about you changing. I don't want you to change. I like you just the way you are. It's about you making an effort, like I did for you. You're a slob and I'm prissy, I know that, but there's a point in the middle where we have to meet. I made an effort to be less prissy for you but you just carried on eating your hot dogs for breakfast and pausing your computer games for, like, three days straight."

"But…"

"Take that fruit bowl I bought for you, for example. Did you ever actually put any fruit in it?"

Cynthia glanced over at the fruit bowl, the one full of M&Ms.

"Yes. Yes, I did. It's full of fruit right now."

"Cynthia. There's no fruit in that fruit bowl."

"There is. There's bananas and…and grapes…and…"

"WhatsApp me a photo of it. Right now."

Cynthia knew Alison had her cornered, but several ways out of this sticky situation still flashed across her mind. One of them involved doing a Google image search for bowls of fruit and sending Alison the one that looked most like her own, but she knew this was probably a non-starter. Another possible scenario involved sprinting out of her apartment and down the street to the nearest grocery store. However, it was a very long street, so she wrote this one off too.

"There's no fruit in the bowl," Cynthia miserably conceded.

"You amaze me."

"But I did quit smoking for you."

"Cynthia, you don't get credit for giving up something you shouldn't have been doing in the first place."

"So, is this it then? Is it really over?"

"It's over."

"Oh, god."

"Cynthia…"

But Cynthia could listen to no more. Just as the hot tears began to flow down her flushed cheeks she terminated the call and tossed the phone down. Sensing that all was not well with his pet human, Mashed Potato jumped up onto her lap and started pawing gently at her face. It had been a long time since he had seen Cynthia crying.

Alison's apartment, in complete contrast to her ex's, was a vision of taste and style. She had conducted this conversation with Cynthia while standing on her balcony, looking out towards the airport where she could see the planes flying in and out, something that she loved.

She placed the gleaming white phone in its gleaming white cradle, sighed and then walked across the room, her bare feet lovingly caressed with every step by the Celeb Bali Sand carpet. She flopped down onto the Mackenzie Pearl Queen Plus Sofa, beneath the framed reproduction of the cover of Whitney Houston's eponymous album. She had to admit, she felt rotten. Alison had been hoping it wouldn't come to tears, especially as she and Cynthia had been 'off' anyway.

The trouble was Cynthia looked like a badass, but all that did was belie how sensitive she actually was. She was needy in a relationship. She depended. But also…

The opening synthesised horn stabs of 'I Wanna Dance with Somebody' interrupted Alison's reverie. She reached for her cell and looked at the screen. It was

Audrey. Christ, if Cynthia was needy in a relationship, it was nothing compared to Audrey, Alison was fast discovering. Not being in the mood for any drama right now, Alison gently put the phone down and waited for the ringtone to play out. A minute later, a text came through.

I've had my mother on the fone and I've been cryin all afternoon!!! Where r u???

Alison rolled her eyes. So, yes, Cynthia was sensitive and needy and dependent, but god she was fun! When you were in her company a good time was guaranteed. She was a riot, a blast and a tonic all in one. Her presence didn't drag you down, it hauled you up by your lapels and insisted that you dance. And right there and then, Alison realised she had made a big mistake.

Chapter 15

It was no surprise that, when night did eventually fall, Esperance could not sleep. In fact, even though her eyes were burning with tears and fatigue, she did not even try. She couldn't so much as blink without seeing those two massive, black alien eyes staring back into her own. The worst thing about them was that they were so completely devoid of life. There was no depth there, no sparkle, with no indication of thought processes taking place behind them. And yet when the alien had moved for her it had done so with efficient intelligence.

So while Buki slumbered quietly in his drawer and Godriva snored softly in her bunk, Esperance sat cross-legged on hers with her arms enfolded around her knees and the duvet wrapped around her shoulders. Over and over in her mind she replayed the awful moment when she had first seen *it*.

She remained hunched up in that position for countless hours, thinking, planning and biting her nails. At some point in the early hours her mind and body succumbed and she slumped over and stayed slumped, unmoving, unconscious. She was finally asleep, but it was far from peaceful.

She was in the jungle by the beach, barefoot and alone. It was night, but under the vivid blue sky and the burning stars, she could see clearly. Above the trees, a large pill-shaped craft, metallic, with three oval windows in the side, was projecting a powerful searchlight down through the branches. *They* were looking for her. The craft was silent and its beam intense. And then it found her. Esperance tried to run, but her legs were leaden. She knew that *they* wanted her, and if they caught her they would do terrible things to her.

But where were Godriva and Buki? They had been with her when Esperance had entered the jungle, but now they were gone. Esperance screamed their names. No reply came. She had lost them forever. She started to cry.

She felt her feet leaving the ground. They had her. In her desperation, she screamed and kicked and thrashed. She called out to her sister but heard no response. The trees were passing her by and the craft was getting closer. Then she was inside it. The cell was small, dark and gunmetal grey. All edges were rounded. Esperance could see the outline of a door in the wall, but otherwise the room was featureless. Still sodden with tears, she threw herself at the door and began pounding on it with her fists. The door made a hollow rattling sound as she beat her small, feeble hands against it. It was no good, there was no give there. She stopped pounding and stepped back, but the hollow clanging noise continued. Where was that coming from? What was causing it? The weak lights in the ceiling suddenly extinguished and all that was left was that horrible sound. The sound was all she had now and so she clung onto it, allowing it to guide her back.

She opened her eyes. She was lying on her side on her bunk, in the foetal position. She could just about see Godriva on the opposite side of the room, still sleeping. Buki was still in his drawer, oblivious to the world. But the noise – the hollow clanging sound – was still with her. It had accompanied her back from the pit of her dream. Esperance was confused. Where was that coming from? And then, with grim horror, she realised.

It was the alien. The alien was trying the grille above its cell again. It was attempting to break out and the noise was travelling up through the vents, all the way to Esperance and Godriva's bunkroom. She looked up to the corner of the room. She hadn't noticed it before, but there was a small grille there. That's where the noise was coming from. Her cruel imagination kicked in once again and tortured her with an image of long, grey, bony fingers wrapping around the grille and pushing it through, sending it crashing to the floor. Then the alien creature in its monstrous, unholy entirety emerged through the tiny open space, its limbs unfolding, its large head appearing last. It was here now, in the same tiny room as Esperance, regarding her with its huge, black, lifeless eyes.

And still the hollow clanging nose continued.

Esperance folded herself up under her duvet, tucking her knees under her chin and clamping her hands over her ears. It began as a whisper...

"Please stop please stop please stop please stop please stop please stop..."

But the whisper grew louder and louder and louder, until Esperance, with red hot tears streaming down her face, was crying out: "SHUT UP! JUST STOP IT! SHUT UP!"

Godriva jumped up in her bunk. Buki started howling.

"STOP IT! STOP IT! STOP IT!"

"Esperance? What is wrong?"

"STOP IT! STOP IT! STOP IT!"

Over her sister's voice, Godriva could not hear the clanging noise coming through the vent.

"Sister, you're frightening me. You're frightening Buki. What is wrong?"

Godriva did not know what to do. Esperance had always been the strong one. She had always been the one to take care of business, to comfort Godriva when the tears flowed.

"Esperance? What has happened?"

Esperance's babbling continued, and so Godriva did the only thing she could think of to help. She put her arms around her sister and hugged her close, and as she did so, Buki, her six-month-old baby, started speaking.

"Free me," he whispered. And then again, "Free me."

Esperance and Godriva looked at each other, disbelieving.

"B…Buki?" Godriva stammered.

"Please," whispered the baby. "Free me."

It was not a full-voiced utterance, as Buki's vocal chords had not yet developed fully. It was more of a whisper, the sound of breath being forced out and words being crudely formed by the mouth as it passed.

Godriva, trembling and wide-eyed with terror, pulled herself from her sister's embrace, switched the light on and looked to her son. He was staring back at her through eyes she did not recognise. His own were vague, watery and uncomprehending. These were sharp and focused and were fixed onto her in a way that sent icy ripples down her spine.

"Free me," Buki whispered again, his tiny mouth moving unnaturally as he did so.

Godriva approached the makeshift drawer cot but was afraid to touch him. "Baby?"

And then a cold wave of realisation washed over Esperance. "It's the alien!" she gasped. "The alien is speaking through him!"

Godriva's hands went to her mouth as tears began streaming from her eyes. She wanted to hold her son but the tiny body lying swaddled in towels before her no longer belonged to him.

"You do not need to fear me," Buki whispered.

And then the levee broke. "LET GO OF MY SON,

YOU MONSTER! LET HIM GO!"

Buki's eyes became vague again and he started gabbling. The alien had left him. Esperance and Godriva looked to each other in silence for a moment, waiting for something else to happen. But nothing did, so Godriva, still horrified and shaking, tentatively picked up her baby boy.

"There there, my little man. All over now. It's all over now."

To her great relief Buki seemed completely oblivious to the horror that had just engulfed him. He smiled and dribbled onto his mother's shoulder, apparently content.

And then the clanging began again.

"Oh god no no no no," Esperance frantically jabbered, her mouth curling with fear and disgust. "Come, sister. We can't stay here."

She led Godriva out of the bunkroom. The clanging followed them through the corridor and into the canteen area. It was even louder in there.

"IS THERE NO ESCAPE?" Esperance cried. "IS THERE NO ESCAPE?"

Her hands clenched into tight fists and she dug her fingers into her hair.

"MAKE IT STOP! MAKE IT STOP!"

Buki started screaming in sympathy with his aunt.

**

Even now, with the sun about to come up, exotic stars

were burning brilliantly in the pale sky. They had sought sanctuary on the roof, the only place where the clanging that was echoing through the vents could not follow. Esperance wondered if she would ever feel safe in the bunkroom again. It had ceased to become a haven for her and she now thought of it as nothing more than a cell.

She was wrapped up in a warm duvet, as was Godriva. They were lying next to each other on loungers, holding hands across the divide. Buki was snuggled in the warm folds of his mother's duvet, apparently suffering no ill effects from the earlier traumas.

Thus far, no distant planets or vast spaceships had intruded upon the earthly sky, for which the sisters, already upset enough, were grateful.

"I think we should kill it," Godriva said, as if proposing the murder of an alien was the most normal thing in the world.

Esperance was taken aback. "What? Are you serious, sister?"

"It has no right being here. It does not belong here. It's dangerous."

"But killing it? How would we…?"

"I don't know. But we have to do it. We have no choice." Godriva sounded resolute.

"There is always a choice," said Esperance. "There's been enough killing here already. This site is a graveyard as it is. You did not see what I saw down

203

there. It was a massacre. I will not add to it. I will not let this island turn me into a killer too."

There were a few moments of silence in which Esperance could sense the cogs turning in her sister's mind. Eventually, Godriva, still upset, tired and red-eyed, delivered the results of her considerations.

"Perhaps if we just leave it there and wait until it starves to death," she said. "I mean, it has to eat, right? So let's just grit our teeth and sit it out. After all, we've got enough supplies to last us for six months or more. It hasn't. How long can it possibly last without food? I give it two weeks at the most. Two weeks and it's dead."

Esperance lowered her eyes and shook her head. "We can't stay here. Not for two weeks, not for six months. What if it doesn't die? What if it doesn't even need to eat. We could be stuck here forever. And what if that spaceship comes back? It's not safe here. We have to find a way off this island."

"Until this 'machine' of theirs has been stabilised, we are not going anywhere."

"Then we must stabilise the machine. There's no other way."

"But that means going back down there to do it," Godriva firmly stated. "Can you face that?"

Esperance realised she had just painted herself into a corner. Stabilising the machine meant facing the bloodbath and the alien in the underground lab a second time.

"What has happened to that girl?" she snapped.

"What was her name? Cynthia? Why didn't she tell me about the alien? She must have known! Where is she?"

There were hundreds of possible reasons why this girl from Arizona had not made contact again since. She might have been fired. She might be dead. She might be nothing more than a chess piece herself, establishing contact at the behest of her superiors before being ordered to stand down.

"Perhaps she didn't know," Godriva offered "Perhaps she is being used just as we are."

"You think we are being used?"

"Don't you?"

Esperance didn't respond. Since she and her sister had been let into this mysterious facility, there had been a nagging feeling in her gut, and now her sister had just put it into words. They were being used. They were being played. They were pawns.

"You are right," she conceded. "Why else would they let us in? They did that so that we could stabilise this machine for them, to make it safe so they can return and carry on their experiments."

"So what are we going to do? Sit here and wait for them to speak to us again? To give us further instructions?"

"I don't know."

"We are prisoners," Godriva said. "Until we do what they want and stabilise that machine, they're not going to let us leave."

Esperance twisted under her duvet. For Godriva,

these were just words, but Esperance was the one who would have to put them into action. She was the one who would have to go crawling through the vent over *its* cell, avoiding its grasping alien hands.

"I can't do it," She said. "I can't go back down there. I can't look at it again. I cannot do it."

"We have no choice. We can't stay here and we can't go home. Doing what they want is the only way."

And as if to prove Godriva's point, the earth once again began to shake. Esperance and Godriva gripped each other's hands tightly as Buki began to murmur. The tremor did not last long, however, and the ebbing of the quake brought with it the dawn chorus of the jungle birds from across the plain.

Godriva picked up her baby boy, her gift from the man she loved, and snuggled him under her chin. She was painfully aware that all this fear, anger and uncertainty was being soaked up by her little Buki, as if he were a sponge that was only capable of absorbing negative emotions.

"Shush, shush, beautiful boy," she soothed. "Beautiful boy."

She succeeded in reassuring him, and then she passed him to his aunt.

"You look after him while I go and fetch breakfast," Godriva said. "I'm hungry, and you must be too."

Godriva left, leaving Buki in Esperance's arms. She looked down to see him looking back at her through penetrating eyes. Every muscle in Esperance's body tightened as she realised the alien had him again.

"I can help you," Buki whispered.

"How can you help us?" a frightened Esperance asked.

The baby looked away. Esperance followed its eyes out across the island. Above the jungle, a pill-shaped craft was hovering silently, frozen in the air. Esperance sat bolt upright on her lounger, her body now rigid with terror.

"Wha…wha…what is it?" she stammered.

"Free me, and I will free you."

The mysterious craft then shot up into the sky and vanished, making no sound as it did so but leaving hundreds of frightened birds flapping in its wake.

"W…w…what do you mean?" Esperance fearfully asked.

She turned back to the baby but something had changed. His eyes were his own again and were regarding her innocently.

"B…b…Buki?"

Buki yawned and looked at his aunt with love in his eyes, but still Esperance kept her breath held. She was just about ready to burst into tears when, a few minutes later, Godriva returned, tray in hand.

"I found the Pop-Tarts," Godriva announced. "Sister. Is everything alright?"

Esperance, not wishing to worry her sister any further, opted to say nothing of what had just happened. "Fine. Everything's fine," She replied with a weak smile.

"Okay. Which do you want, strawberry or blueberry? Actually why don't we have one of each?"

Godriva placed the tray down on the little table between the loungers. "Here," she said as she passed a plate and a cup of tea over to her sister. "I wonder if they have Pop-Tarts in South Africa. I hope so."

Esperance said nothing and instead looked back to the distant jungle where she had seen the hovering alien craft. All was as it should be again, and the morning sun was peeking over the canopy of the trees.

"Esperance?" Godriva asked. "Are you sure you're alright? You seem a bit…not yourself."

Esperance was in general not someone to lie, especially to her sister, but there'd been quite enough horror this morning already. "Just looking at the sunrise," she said.

The Pop-Tarts were still warm and smelled enticing, but Esperance didn't feel in the slightest bit hungry after what had just happened. However, out of duty to Godriva, she picked up one of the cream-coloured rectangles and took a nibble. With that first bite, she realised that she was in fact ravenous and devoured the lot in seconds.

Chapter 16

So that's it. I've quit. Elise Diamond called a Central Security meeting and went through the plan, apparently approved by Mr B, to throw the Cynthia Dowley girl under a bus if and when the 'incident', as she called it, goes public. I should have done it when the refugees were allowed to make landfall. Quit, I mean. Not throw Cynthia Dowley under a bus. We all knew what was going to happen when that boat hit shore, and happen it did. That was the first line I crossed and I've crossed quite a few more since, so I'm making a stand. I'm not going to be party to pinning thirty deaths on some innocent girl and ruining her life just so the big boss man can save his own Texan ass. The lot of them can go hang. I'm through.

Journal entry dated 11thJanuary, 2018.

***

Cynthia could feel her life unravelling around her.

Firstly, there was the promotion. She was in way over her head in her new position, especially given what Al Leon and Champagne Star – or whatever the hell their real names were – had just told her. Was she really about to be hurled into the centre of a media shit storm? Hung out to dry for all the world – and, worst of all, her parents – to judge and condemn? Secondly, there were the two refugee women and the baby. Cynthia would not be able to live with herself if she simply walked away and abandoned them to their fate inside the lab site. And thirdly, there was Alison.

So Cynthia had resorted to doing what she always did during a crisis: hiding under the duvet. The tears had long since come and gone, but she was pretty sure there would be more. Also, she couldn't get her head around the fact that such an awful cliché could be so true: that you don't know what you've got until it's gone.

Why didn't I just try harder? her inner voice whined. *She never asked that much of me. She just wanted me to take better care of myself. Why didn't I do it? Then I wouldn't be lying here feeling so fucking rotten. It's not fair.*

Mashed Potato, bored and hungry, jumped up onto the bed and started pawing at the human-shaped lump beneath the duvet.

"Hey, boy," Cynthia murmured from her cocoon. "Is it dinnertime already?"

The cat purred enthusiastically.

"Hey. I know a solicitation purr when I hear one. You

210

can't fool me."

Undeterred, Mashed Potato continued his campaign of harassment until Cynthia could feel her walls crumbling.

"Okay. Okay. You win. I'm coming."

Mashed Potato jumped from the bed and led his bedraggled human into the kitchen. Still bleary-eyed and teary-eyed, Cynthia spotted something on the floor. It was a note that had been pushed under the door. She picked it up and read it.

Meet me at Paulette's Pancakes and Ice Cream at 5.

"Oh god. What now?"

***

Esperance had heard it said that it only takes three days to adjust to a new normality. While she and her sister were sitting in the living block's canteen room – Esperance sipping from a mug of strong, black coffee while Godriva was feeding Buki – she suddenly realised that she had been ignoring the views out of the windows. The canteen was light and airy and offered panoramic vistas of the beautiful landscape beyond the facility grounds.

She barely noticed the three blue savages who had crossed the plain from the jungle and were now pacing back and fore just beyond the fence. They had already become nothing more than a part of the scenery, it seemed.

Esperance was hoping that the coffee she was cradling in her jittery hands would help bring her around a little after her hellish night. She felt cornered, as though she, her sister and her baby nephew had been caught in a perfect pincer movement. Somewhere below them, in the catacombs of the facility, amongst the strewn corpses, was a living breathing alien. A being from a distant world whose intentions may be unknown but Esperance was for now assuming were malign, or else why would it be imprisoned? Above them was a window to the cold, far reaches of the universe. Or was it a doorway? Either way, there were planets up there, and spaceships, which meant more aliens. And out there on the plain were giant blue savages who could run like demons and lived only to kill.

They were flanked on all sides and the only pathway out, the only glimmer of hope yet offered to them, rested on one of them stabilising this mysterious machine. Despite everything she had already endured, Esperance accepted that this job was hers. She could not send her sister to do it.

Esperance looked on as Godriva tended to Buki. Only two days previously she had feared her sister's spirit had been broken following the death of the boy from the boat at the hands of the blue savages. But now Esperance herself felt she was teetering on the edge of madness, and it terrified her.

"Are you okay?" Godriva asked.

Esperance was caught by surprise. "Yes. Just thinking."

"About going back down there?"

"Yes. About going back down there."

She had very briefly considered asking her sister to venture down into the depths, so that she would be spared the horror of facing that creature a second time. But no. How could she do such a thing? How could she be so selfish? For a start, Godriva had to stay with Buki. If Esperance sent Godriva in her place and something happened to her, Esperance would never be able to forgive herself. Not only would she have lost her sister, she would have deprived a tiny baby of its mother. Furthermore, she wanted, if possible, to spare her beloved sister the horror that she herself had endured when she had looked into *its* eyes.

Her love for Godriva had made the decision for her. Esperance was prepared to venture back down into the bloodbath beneath their feet so that her sister could spend the rest of her life free of that trauma.

"I'll do it today," Esperance said flatly. "Then they can come and rescue us."

"What? Are you sure?" Godriva was taken aback. She had not expected her sister to announce that she was venturing back down there quite so soon.

"It's the only way," Esperance shrugged.

Godriva reached across the table and squeezed Esperance's hand.

"Oh, my sister. Are you sure? Are you really sure?"

"Yes. We have to do what needs to be done, and we have to do it quickly. The girl from Arizona said if this machine down there blows then it could take the whole island with it. The sooner I do it, the sooner we can get out of here."

"And when rescue comes, we can tell them we're from South Africa, and hopefully they'll take us there."

"Perhaps."

"Oh, Esperance. I love you."

Esperance leaned forward and rested her forehead against Godriva's.

"I love you too, sister."

Esperance's nose crinkled and an expression of distaste wafted across her face.

"Esperance? What's the matter?" Godriva asked.

"I think Buki needs changing."

Godriva smiled a little. "I think you're right."

She laid her baby on his back on the table in order to change his nappy.

"Free me," he whispered.

Esperance and Godriva jumped back, knocking their chairs over, sending coffee flying, although thankfully not over the baby.

"Free me," Buki said again, his vague eyes coming into sharp focus.

"Buki?" Godriva asked. She was trembling with shock and her eyes looked like they were trying to force their way out of her skull.

Buki's head turned to the side to face Esperance. "You can help me."

Esperance tried to speak, to answer, but the words would not come. "I…I…"

Godriva's hands went up to her mouth as her sense of sanity thrashed and flailed.

"There is no need to fear me," Buki said, intelligence and understanding burning in his eyes. "I have no wish to harm you. My only desire is to return to my own people. You can help me to do this."

Still Esperance could not speak. She looked to Godriva who shrieked: "WHAT HAVE YOU DONE TO MY SON? WHAT HAVE YOU DONE TO BUKI?"

Slowly, horrifyingly, Buki's head turned to face his mother.

"I am merely speaking through him. He is unharmed. He is unaware of…"

"Why don't you speak through one of us?" Esperance demanded. "Or to us directly, if you are psychic?"

Buki's head turned back towards her. "The child's mind is open," he whispered. "Yours is not."

Godriva, too terrified even to approach or touch her own son, the baby she had brought into the world, the precious gift left to her by her beloved Benjamin, raged, "GET OUT OF MY BABY! GET OUT OF HIM! GIVE ME BACK MY SON!"

"They gave me a name: Victor."

By now Godriva was all but lost in madness. Esperance rushed to her and held her.

"I can help you escape this place, but there isn't much time. The quakes are coming much more frequently now. The Machine is nearing meltdown."

"I can stabilise the machine," Esperance snarled. "They told me how to do it."

"No," Buki whispered. "Rebooting the facility as they told you would only restore power to it. It would not stabilise it. Only I can do that."

"Liar!"

"The quakes will keep on happening as The Machine approaches its end. You'll see."

By now Godriva had her face buried in Esperance's shoulder. Esperance felt hot tears running down it.

"Make it stop," Godriva whimpered like a frightened child. "Make it stop."

Buki fixed Godriva with a cold, hard stare. "I can feel your pain," he whispered. "You yearn for Benjamin. You want him back."

By uttering that name, Esperance understood that the alien had struck deep into the heart of her sister. She tried to keep her arms wrapped around Godriva but she wriggled free.

"How can you know that?" Godriva demanded as she clutched at her short hair with her fingers. "HOW?"

"I feel what you feel. I know what you know."

"Don't you ever say that name!" she snapped. "Don't you dare!"

"Do not fear me. I mean no harm to you."

"Why are you a prisoner?" Esperance asked. "What did you do?"

The baby, still lying on its back on the table, fixed Esperance with its unnerving gaze. "I am not a prisoner," he whispered.

"You are locked in a cell. I saw it with my own eyes. Why?"

"When the test subjects rampaged, I was placed in this cell by the scientists for my own protection. If they had not done so, my fate would have been the same as theirs. They saved my life."

"LIAR!" Godriva screamed.

"I have no reason to lie," said the being in possession of Buki.

***

Paulette's Pancakes and Ice Cream was one of Cynthia's regular haunts, so she knew it well. The sun was just starting to set when she got off the bus, and she was a little early, so, with her stomach knotting, she hung around on the opposite street corner and waited for the appointed time. She could see indistinct human shapes through the steamy window but could not identify anyone. A lone man approached from sidewalk east and went in. He looked like a company rep type. Could it have been him who slipped the note under her door?

Cynthia zipped up her leather jacket to insulate herself from the winter chill. Then she pulled a beanie hat – complete with Sumo Cyco logo, of course – from her pocket and slipped it over her mohawk. Now suitably warm, she retrieved her cell, hit the side button and brought the screen to life. She tapped on the Twitter icon and searched #SpaceWurd. What she saw was not good; share price falling, commercial space flights delayed. But Twitter was not where she needed to be looking. There were websites and forums out there dedicated to conspiracy theories. That's where she'd find all the chatter about the East Africa lab and the accident. But standing on a street corner, leaning against a lamp post, was not the time for that. Tomorrow, maybe.

She looked for Matt's Instagram. Just the usual pics of him with his wife and kids. Nothing about work. But then, there never was. That was a subject Matt never broached on social media.

She put her phone away and wondered how long this was going to take exactly. She was supposed to be on duty that evening and had to be at the airport at seven-thirty to catch the plane. The thought of walking back into the top tier with all its murky machinations made her stomach churn.

Screw it. She'd had enough of loitering so she crossed the road and entered the diner. The first thing she saw was Neal Terry in his trademark flat cap sitting at a table with two young children. He turned around as

218

the bell on the door chimed and waved her over.

"I'm going to go ahead and assume you've been twisting and turning at night, wondering what the hell's going on at the port. Well, get yourself some ice cream cos I'm gonna tell ya."

***

Esperance pulled open the hatch and gazed down into its maw. It was a long drop to the airlock. She shuddered at the thought of what awaited her.

It's a ladder that leads to hell, she thought.

"Sister. Are you sure about this?"

Godriva was standing at her side with Buki, swaddled in a towel, cradled in her good arm.

"Not really, but what choice do we have?"

"Promise me something."

"What?"

Godriva took her sister's arm and gently pulled her around so that they were eye to eye.

"Don't go looking for the alien, don't even think about helping it and, whatever you do, don't talk to it. Just reboot the power like the girl from Arizona said and then come back to us. Forget about that thing that keeps taking my baby. It doesn't deserve your help."

"How *can* I forget about it?"

"Once you've done what the girl said, they'll come for us. That's the only thing that matters. Leave the alien where it is, locked in its cell where it cannot harm us."

"I have no desire to harm you," Buki whispered.

Godriva almost dropped him in her shock. "No! Not again! Not again!"

"Quickly! Put him down!" Esperance cried.

Godriva laid Buki in his towel on the ground. He turned his head and stared hard at his mother and his auntie.

"They won't come for you," he whispered. "They lied."

***

Cynthia wasn't a lover of ice cream as she had sensitive teeth, so she got herself coffee and pancakes instead and took a seat.

"This is André and this is Juniper," Neal said, nodding towards the little boy sitting beside him and the little girl Cynthia had just slid in next to. "Say hello," he told them, and they did.

"Hey there," Cynthia awkwardly replied. She was far better around cats than kids. "So what you got there?"

Juniper – *such a gorgeous name,* Cynthia thought – was colouring. "It's a unicorn," the little girl said without looking up. "I wanted to colour her gold but I haven't got gold, so I'm colouring her yellow."

Cynthia reckoned she was around four years old. "Nice," she said. "I like unicorns, but I couldn't eat a whole one."

"Yeah, Juniper's a regular artist, alright," Neal said

with a sweep of a large hand. "And what do you call yourself, André?"

"A gamer," replied the boy, also without looking up. He was perhaps three years older than his sister and was staring intensely at the portable console he was holding inches from his face.

"No shit? Me too," Cynthia remarked. Then a whole handful of pennies dropped. "Oh. Sorry. I mean; really? Me too."

Neal just chuckled. "So there you have it. A gamer. The future's in safe hands. How are the pancakes?"

"Divine."

"Glad to hear it. Help you grow up big n strong, just like me. So, guess what? You won't be seeing me on the plane again anytime soon. I quit."

"What? You're kidding? Why?"

"I'll get to that presently. Well, you going to ask me why I had you come meet me here, or do I have to wait all day?"

Despite Cynthia barely knowing him, she liked this Neal Terry guy. He was unflappable, rather like Gene back at the hot dog stand. Also, he seemed to possess a hearty quantity of cynicism, a quality Cynthia always admired. Oh, and he had an honest face too, and right now that honest face was regarding her closely.

"So, why'd you bring me here?" she dutifully asked.

"Good question. Basically, a steaming great pile of horse manure is about to hit an industrial-sized fan, and you're the one who's going to get covered in it. Now, I

221

like to think that as a human being I'm pretty decent. I have morals. I have scruples. And for the most part, I like the people I work with – or did work with – and I don't want any of them to be standing there naked when the shit starts flying."

At the mention of the S-word, Cynthia looked to André and Juniper.

"What? You think they ever listen to what I'm saying?" Neal laughed. "Also, I'm hopeful that once I've told you what I'm about to tell you, you'll then go and tell somebody else, who'll tell somebody else and so forth, until everybody knows but nobody knows where it first came from. Make sense?"

Cynthia nodded, then said, "Those two Men in Black dudes called on me at home. They said pretty much the same thing, that I'm being lined up to take the fall."

"Interesting."

"Yeah. They said they've seen it all before and they wanted to warn me. They said I should start writing down everything that happens to cover myself."

"Good advice. That's what I've been doing. I keep a journal and everything that happens at the port goes in there."

"But why would they do that? Why would they use me like that at the port and then try to warn me about being set up?"

"Just because they're government doesn't mean they ain't decent human beings. Perhaps they just wanted to help a girl out. But all that aside, I know there's at least one head-spinner of a question you're dying to ask me, so go ahead."

"Is there really an alien on the site?"

"Yes. There's an alien at the East Africa lab."

Cynthia was finding the mouthful of pancake she had just taken hard to swallow. Not because it wasn't tasty – it most certainly was – but because a fellow human being had just confirmed to her that there really were such things as aliens and one of them was already here, on Earth, at a site she had CCTV access to.

"Have you seen it?"

"No. I'm pretty sure only Elise Diamond and her top two or three minions have CCTV access to the alien's holding area. But it's there alright, no question about that."

"But how do you know? I mean, how can you be so sure if you've never seen it?"

"Because without the alien, there would be no facility."

Completely oblivious to the gravitas of the conversation taking place right next to them, André and Juniper continued entertaining themselves.

"What do you mean?" Cynthia asked.

"What I mean is that the alien is overseeing the whole operation. Sure, the SpaceWurd corporation is planning on sending astronauts on long distance missions into deep space, but forget all this talk of Mars and Europa. That isn't even the half of it. Actually, it isn't even one percent of it. These astronauts were headed off to a distant part of the universe, millions of light years away. They were supposed to be working with an alien civilisation far in advance of our own."

"Working with?"

"Basically, they were envoys. Ambassadors. They were going to be mankind's representatives in another galaxy."

"Jesus."

"No. He's got nothing to do with it."

"Daddy. Can I have another shake?"

"Not until you've finished the one you've got, Juniper."

Juniper returned to her colouring.

"So what went wrong? Was it the storm, like they said?"

"God, no. All the important stuff was taking place deep underground. The storm couldn't touch it. It was the alien who screwed everything up."

"What? Why?"

"Because, as it turns out, this alien civilisation has been taking us for a big hellzapoppin' ride this whole time. You heard talk of The Machine?"

"Yeah," Cynthia said, "Those two CIA dudes said something about it."

"They ain't CIA."

"They ain't?"

"No. They're government, but they ain't CIA?"

"Oh."

"Oh indeed. So, The Machine is actually what this

whole great big shit show has been about. Say, you going to finish that?"

Cynthia had pushed the remains of her pancakes aside.

"Um. No. Go ahead."

Neal pulled the plate over the table. "Just don't tell my wife," he said with a wink.

Bemused, Cynthia watched him spoon a pile into his mouth and savour it.

"Man, these are good. We have a rule at home. No sugar Monday to Friday. My wife's on a weight-loss drive, which means we all are."

"Sounds like hell."

"It is. So, you know the CERN place in Switzerland where they collide atoms and stuff like that?"

"Yeah."

"Well, that's a child's toy compared to what our fricking Machine can do."

"Daddy!"

"I said 'fricking', honey."

A bored waitress came over. "Can I get you guys anything else?"

"We're good for now, thank you," said Neal without taking his eyes away from Cynthia. Then he continued, "So, the aliens gave the government the plans for The Machine, along with a few components that mankind has yet to even imagine, let alone invent. But the government couldn't risk sinking such a huge amount of public money into it, because a sum that big would be noticed by waaaay too many people and questions would get asked, so they brought in Byron Wurd. Made a deal with him. He builds The Machine for the government, the government lets him in on the technology they get from the aliens, he becomes even richer."

"So, it's just business, huh?"

"That old cliché," Neal replied with a smirk.

"So, when you talk about 'government', does that mean Trump's in on this?"

Neal almost spat out a mouthful of coffee.

"God, no! You think the president – any president – gets let near any of this? No way, sister. Presidents come and go and they don't want some raging narcissist like Trump shooting his big orange mouth off about it after he's lost his job. No, when I refer to 'the government' I'm talking about the people who *really* run the country. The big fish. The ones who determine the direction this country takes in the decades and centuries to come, not the minnows who bleat on about building fences."

"Okaaaay."

"I can see you're sceptical and frankly I don't blame you. I'd be the same if some doofus like me sat down and started reeling off crap like this. But what I'm passing on to you now is what I've seen and heard over the last few years."

"Daddy, I've finished. Look."

Juniper held up her unicorn picture, now fully coloured, for her father to see.

"Hey, girl! That's good enough to frame! One day it'll be worth millions!"

Smiling proudly, Juniper showed it to Cynthia.

"Wow. That's pretty damn…erm…darn good. You're a better artist than I am. Go Juniper! So what does The Machine actually do?" Cynthia asked, turning back to Neal.

"Well now, that's the interesting part. I hope you brought yourself some clean underwear."

***

Godriva was on her hands and knees in the dirt, crying over the baby that was no longer hers.

"What do you mean by that? Why won't they come for us?" she cried.

"They do not care about you. All they care about is The Machine. But I can help you escape this island."

"How? How can you help us?" Esperance asked, her arms wrapped tightly around the shoulders of her sister.

"I know what it is you want more than anything else. What you both want."

The baby looked directly into Godriva's eyes. "You wish to leave this place and start a new life elsewhere…"

He then faced Esperance. "…and you wish to return home."

Godriva fixed Esperance with an accusing stare. "Sister? Is this true?"

Esperance, caught unawares, had no answer.

"I...I..." she stammered.

On this, the alien was correct. Although Esperance had not admitted as such, not even to herself, the strongest yearning in the deepest recesses of her heart was to be reunited with her mother and father. For all its chaos and its dangers, she longed to return to her home, to Burundi.

Buki's eyes were still intensely focused. "We can take you wherever you want to go in the world, in mere moments."

"We?"

"When you free me, I will stabilise The Machine and then activate it. This will allow my people to come here, to Earth, instantaneously."

***

"No. Freakin'. Way."

"Way," Neal nodded grimly.

The look on his face told Cynthia that everything Neal had just said, he meant. He wasn't kidding around here, this was really happening. This was the real deal. The world was about to change, and among the tiny bodies that would be hurled into the maelstrom was her own and the ones belonging to the two sisters still stuck in the East Africa facility. Oh, and the baby.

Neal chuckled as he noticed Cynthia's mouth moving with no actual words being produced. "You see," he continued, "they've always been here, the aliens, the 'greys', call them what you will; observing, sometimes interfering, sometimes even crashing."

"You mean Roswell."

"I do."

"So that actually happened. Like, for real."

"It did."

"Groovy."

"And sometimes abducting too, but that's a whole other plateful of insanity. But these are all – how shall I put this? – away teams, advance scouts. They're the ones who've been preparing the ground for the main event."

"The main event?"

"Yeah. But before I tell you 'bout that, I need to tell you what happened the first time The Machine was fired up."

"Okay."

"As far as the people on the ground knew – by which I mean the scientists and engineers and test subjects – The Machine was supposed to open a doorway that would allow the test subjects – the astronauts – to travel to the alien's world on a UFO that was already here on Earth, pretty much instantaneously."

"Wow!"

"I know. That's what all the body mods were for, so they'd survive it. So the first time The Machine was fired up, it was only supposed to be a trial run, a test. But the alien lied about how it works. What he didn't say was that when we fire our Machine up, the aliens on the other side of the universe also fire theirs up, and the beams meet in the middle to create a wormhole."

"Yowers! So what's the difference between a doorway and a wormhole?"

"A doorway would just allow the ship carrying our astronauts through and then close again. A wormhole is permanent."

"Okay. That's pretty scary."

"Yeah. So when we activated our Machine, the test subjects were all in stasis as part of a trial run. And when the aliens fired up theirs, our systems couldn't handle it and went haywire, and *that's* what fried the astronauts' brains – *not* the hurricane."

Cynthia exhaled deeply and sank back in her seat. This was a lot to take in. Too much, actually. "So, the wormhole? What's it for? I mean, what's the endgame here?"

"Remember me asking you if you brought clean underwear? Well, there's an armada coming, and I'm not talking about piddly little flying saucers here either. Something huge. Basically, the time has come for the aliens to formerly declare their presence, and this is how they're doing it."

"When you say an 'armada', you don't mean, like, an invasion, do you?"

Now it was Neal's turn to sink back into his very uncomfortable plastic seat. "Your guess is as good as mine," he said with a shrug.

"But what are we gonna do? I mean, everybody? The whole world. What are we gonna do?"

Neal was nonchalant, but it was the nonchalance of someone who had accepted the fact he was powerless.

"Who can say? In the whole entire history of mankind, nothing like this has ever happened before. There's no manual for it. It could be every man for himself, or it could be pull together as one and help each other through it. I'm hoping for the latter, but I sure ain't betting on it."

Cynthia's mind raced with approximately one million complex calculations per second, and through the swirling vortex of her thoughts, two things remained clear; one, she wanted Alison by her side. Preferably forever. And two, she had to help the sisters and the baby back at the facility. She could not – *would* not – just abandon them. And, as it happened, she had a plan.

Cynthia stood up suddenly. "I gotta go," she said. "There's something I gotta put right."

Juniper looked up from her colouring. "Bye bye," she said, and gave a little wave.

André grunted without lifting his eyes from his game.

"Bye, Juniper," Cynthia said. "Keep up the good work there. You're gonna be a famous artist one day. And André, well…I don't think you're even listening to me anyway, so…"

She hoped, deeply and sincerely, that these two children were going to be alright, given everything Neal had just told her. Then Neal took hold of her by the

231

wrist, but not hard or aggressively.

"You okay?" he asked with sincere concern.

"Honest answer? Not really."

"Don't go doing anything foolish, now," Neal warned. "There's always the slim hope that everything will work out fine in the end."

"I hear you," Cynthia, still in a daze, replied. "And thank you. I mean it. Thank you so much. Be safe."

"May The Force be with you, or something," Neal replied.

True love, like a fatal accident, often happens when one is looking the other way, and as if to prove it, when Cynthia stumbled out of the diner door she ran straight into Alison.

"Hey! There you are! I've been looking all over for you!" Alison was smiling, relieved to have found her friend, her love. "Why haven't you been answering your..." Then she noticed the mix of shock and confusion on Cynthia's face. "Hey, what's wrong? What's happened?"

Cynthia threw her arms around the befuddled love of her life. "Oh, god! Please don't leave me again! Please don't leave me again!"

Alison warmly returned the embrace as passer-by looked on. "It's okay. I'm not going anywhere. You were right about Audrey. That was a terrible mistake. You and I belong together, like..."

Cynthia clasped her hands around Alison's face and stared hard into her eyes. "Have you got your car? Can you drive me home and then to the spaceport? I need to save someone's life."

Alison was understandably blindsided by this. "Um…okay…" was all she could manage.

***

Godriva placed her forehead against Esperance's.

"Promise you'll come back to me, sister. Promise."

"I promise," said Esperance.

"And then stay with me and Buki, no matter what."

"Sister…I…"

"I can't go back to Burundi, not after it took my Benjamin from me, and I can't go on to South Africa alone. I need you, and so does Buki. Please stay with us."

Esperance knew that she had no choice. Her sister's need was far greater than her own.

"I'll come," she promised as she squeezed Godriva's hand. "Now, I'll do this as quickly as I can. Wish me luck."

Godriva watched as Esperance descended the ladder. Then she did something that she was not especially wont to do; she prayed.

***

Cynthia crashed in through her apartment door, closely followed by a thoroughly confused Alison. Cynthia had

233

attempted to give her now 'on' girlfriend an account of what was going down at the spaceport and the East Africa lab facility, but it had been rambling and nonsensical.

"I need my new top tier SmartCard," Cynthia said as she hauled it out from down the back of the battered sofa.

"Wait. You keep your SmartCard down the back of the couch?" Alison asked, incredulous. "Something that important?"

"Yep."

"Do you keep anything else down there that I need to know about?"

"Only my passport."

"Please tell me you're not serious!"

Before Cynthia could respond to this, a bleary-eyed Mashed Potato staggered in from the direction of the bedroom. He had clearly only just woken up.

"Hey, gorgeous boy!" Alison squealed. "Come here to mommy! Have you missed me? Have you?"

At any other time, Cynthia would have reminded Alison that Mashed Potato only had one mommy, and it was her. But right now, she was focused on just one thing: getting the sisters and the baby off that damn island before all hell broke loose.

"Come on. We gotta go."

"Can't I at least have five minutes with my beautiful boy here?" Alison was rubbing her nose against the cat's.

"'Fraid not. Time's a-wastin'. Let's hustle."

"Hey! Are those M&Ms in the fruit bowl I gave you?"

***

Esperance was back in the shaft, the one that housed the grille that ran over the cell that contained the alien. She stared ahead into the flickering light, her arms shaking, her flesh cold, her stomach writhing. She had no doubt that the creature already knew she was here.

On her hands and knees and with her head pressed against the low ceiling, she forced her quivering body forward as silently as possible. As she moved, her eyes remained fixed on the grille up ahead. She remembered that it was the third one along. She expected at any moment to see the alien's spindly fingers slip through the bars like the legs of a spider, as she had the last time.

Esperance passed over the first grille. She considered closing her eyes and shuffling forward as fast as her knees would allow until she reached the end of the vent, thus curtailing the horror of the situation, but this would have made too much noise, and so she continued her tortuously slow progress which by now had taken her over the second grille.

Her mind was in full flow now, churning out ghastly image after ghastly image; the alien staring up at her, the alien grasping at her through the bars, the alien whispering to her as she passed overhead. And still the

235

lights kept flickering.

She didn't want to stop and lose her momentum, but her body rebelled. The third grille, the one over the alien's cell, was directly ahead. The creature's huge dark eyes forced themselves into her mind. Was *it* doing that, or was she? Esperance reminded herself of what was at stake. *We have to get off this island,* she stated firmly and noiselessly. *We have to get off this island. We have to get off this island.*

With this mantra circulating in her brain, she closed her eyes, readied herself to put on a burst of speed, and…

She could feel it through her hands, which were spread out web-like on the floor of the vent. It was another earthquake. Within seconds, the shaft was rattling and swaying.

Not now! Not now!

Esperance had a vision of the shaft collapsing into the creature's cell, trapping her in there with it. She had to move and move now, so she went for it. As she was crawling over the grille she made the mistake of peeking and saw the alien's face pressed up against it, its mouth a black, gaping hole as if it were screaming at her. Esperance herself screamed and sped on, sick with panic, her mind bordering on madness. When she reached the end of the shaft she realised that she was still screaming.

There was a ladder down and so she took it, all but crashing onto the shuddering floor below. She was breathing hard and her face was hot with sweat. She wanted to cry out but she daren't, so she stifled it. The whole site was shaking and rattling and full of noise. She took a deep breath and tried to focus. To her left was a door and to her right a service corridor. It was cold, narrow and grey, the same pallid colour as the alien's flesh. Here too the light came in intermittent blasts, and along the length of the ceiling and the walls ran dozens of tubes and cables.

Follow the cables. Esperance remembered the instruction from the voice through the loudspeaker system the day before. *Follow the cables.*

She ran and ran fast, struggling to keep her footing as the ground rumbled beneath her feet. But she did not slow down, because she knew that every step was carrying her further away from that thing. It was an abomination that had no right to be alive, Esperance decided, no right to be here. Such things as this did not exist back in Burundi, or anywhere else for that matter. Giant blue savages, mysterious planets, spaceships, aliens, they only existed here on this...what? Supernatural island? Is that what it was? Supernatural? Here, nightmare piled on top of nightmare on top of nightmare. Would they all miraculously cease the instant a boat took Esperance and her sister away? Or, better still, a helicopter? Esperance decided that they would.

The ground stopped shaking and the rattling noise subsided, leaving only silence. Esperance thanked God, although she did not believe in him anymore. The tunnel was long, but at last she came to a right turn, just as the girl on the other side of the world had promised. She took it and stopped dead. Before her, in the flickering light, stood a large grey door. Why was everything down here grey?

The door doesn't lock, so you should be able to just walk in.

So the voice through the loudspeaker had said. Esperance turned the handle and, yes, the door opened. She stepped inside. Here too, the light was intermittent. The room was small and smelled of dust and neglect. Esperance could swear that this tight space was getting tighter. She closed her eyes and tried to push the image of the alien from her mind.

What did the girl say? A row of six big switches on the wall; five black and one red. They should all be in the up position. Push them all to the down position, in sequence from left to right, with the red switch last. Then push them all back up in the same sequence, and that should restore power to the machine.

Approximately ninety seconds later the lights came back online and the cables lining the walls and ceiling started humming. Esperance now had the comfort of knowing that she did not have to return the way she had come. She did not have to traverse the shaft over the alien's cell. She could just walk out of here.

Minding the instructions, she followed the tunnel back until she came to the ladder she had all but fallen down minutes earlier. And there was the door that the girl from Arizona had told her to look out for. It too was grey and featureless, save for a little black box where a knob or a handle would normally be. Esperance reached down the front of her vest and pulled out the SmartCard that had been hanging around her neck. She tapped it against the little black box and heard a locking mechanism release. She tentatively pushed the door open and was greeted by carnage.

There were three dead bodies strewn about the floor and blood everywhere. Lying across Esperance's path was a woman in an engineer's overall. She was a large lady, black, and her throat was torn open. There was a huge smear of blood across the floor that ended underneath her, indicating she had been dragged. The shredded flesh on her hands and forearms suggested she had put up a hell of a fight before she died. Also, her eyes were still open and staring in Esperance's direction. She looked away. The air down here was cold, so there wasn't much of a smell coming from the bodies, which was a relief.

Beyond the remains of the woman in the overalls were those of two of the female test subjects, both naked, both ripped and torn. Esperance reckoned that they were at least six foot tall.

The floor was criss-crossed with giant bloody footprints, obviously left behind by the male test subjects. Esperance wondered if the black woman had died trying to protect the two blue women from the rampaging men. But then, wouldn't the female test subjects have been turned into savages too? Perhaps they had killed the black woman before being themselves set upon by their male counterparts.

Esperance, concentrating on not making eye contact with any of the dead, negotiated her way around the strewn bodies to the centre of the room where there stood a huge metal pod. This one was quite unlike the pods she had already seen and looked like it had come straight out of a sci-fi horror movie, with hundreds of wires and cables feeding into it from the ceiling above. It was gunmetal grey and opaque, save for a small window where, presumably, whoever was in it was able to see out. Timidly, she leant over and peered through the glass. There was no one in the pod, for which Esperance was grateful.

She wondered how many more bodies she would find. The loudspeaker girl said there had been a total of twenty staff and ten female test subjects here. It was a gruesome thought. She approached the next door, which was still sealed. With SmartCard in hand, she wondered what lay beyond it. More victims of the blue savages? Almost certainly. The alien? Esperance shuddered at the thought. She was hoping to find her way back to daylight without seeing the face of that thing again. She tapped the little black box and opened the door.

***

The entourage entered first – the personal assistant, the press secretary, the attorney, the security advisor, the government attaché – with Byron Wurd following behind, as ever sporting his trademark Stetson and cowboy boots. He was known for never cracking a smile, and tonight the look on his craggy face suggested he was not about to buck this particular trend.

Having his entourage go before him was a policy of his. It gave the impression that something important was about to happen, that the person following in their wake was not a person at all, but something far more.

He had picked up this little trick from Adolf Hitler. Or, more specifically, from a biography of Adolf Hitler. When the future Führer was still nothing more than a rabble-rousing party leader, he would not make his appearance at a speaking event until his armed guards had gone in ahead and parted the crowd, thus giving the impression that a major figure was about to enter the frame. A man of power.

Mr B liked this. He admired Hitler's grip on the psychology of the crowd. Unfortunately, it was not the only thing he admired about the former German chancellor.

"Latest?"

When Byron Wurd spoke, things happened. Necks were craned so that aghast stares could be aimed in his direction. Wide-eyed looks were exchanged. Then, the spaceport administrator, Elise Diamond, appeared at his side.

"It's begun," said Elise coldly. "One of the refugee women has seen Victor. Victor's been communicating with them via the baby. It's only a matter of time now."

If anyone had been watching closely they'd have seen Elise's lip curl with the utterance of the word 'refugee.' Cynthia was already convinced that Elise was a psychopath, and she'd only worked one shift in the top tier control room.

"Is there visual?"

With an icy hand, Elise tapped on the shoulder of the man sitting at the nearest workstation.

"You. Take your SmartCard out," she ordered.

"What? My SmartCard? Why?" asked the underling, whose name was Mostin. He had not been prepped for this impromptu visit from the head of the company and so had been caught on the hop.

"Just do it," an exasperated Elise snapped.

Mostin did as he was told. He pulled his SmartCard from the slot on his workstation, leaving his screens blank. Then he hung it around his neck on its lanyard. He winced as Elise leaned over him, inserting her own Priority 1 SmartCard. Then she typed in her password. Mostin made a point of looking away as she did so.

"Okay. Ready," said Elise to the boss man.

"Everyone! Everyone! Attention, please!" Byron Wurd hollered in his cowboy drawl.

The workers at their workstations all turned to look at him.

"I would just like to remind you of the non-disclosure

242

agreements in your contracts. What you are about to see does not leave this building! Understand?"

He was answered by a lot of nodding and a few nervous gulps.

"Okay," Byron said to Elise.

Elise again tapped Mostin on the shoulder. "In the CCTV menu for the East Africa lab site you'll see options that were not previously available to you. Find the one entitled 'Victor' and bring it up."

Mostin did so and then there it was, on the big screen, as if it was the most normal thing in the world.

Mostin stared in stunned silence. Various colleagues inhaled sharply. The press secretary gasped and clasped a hand over his mouth. The personal assistant's mouth dropped open. The security advisor dumbly uttered, "Judas fuckin' Priest." And the government attaché said and did nothing. He'd seen it all before.

The image was pin-sharp, HD quality. This only served to make the thing that every pair of eyes in the room was now fixed on all the more grotesque. It was an alien.

"Marvellous," said Mr B.

With his back straight and his jaw thrust forward, a hint of a smile threatened momentarily to flicker across the old man's face, so he suppressed it.

***

This room, vast and bright, was a gym. There were

running machines, exercise bikes, cross-trainers, workout mats, free weights, overhead bars and more bloody footprints criss-crossing the floor. Also, there were several ECG machines scattered about, much like the ones Esperance used back in the hospital, only far more expensive-looking.

Esperance decided that a gym could come in very handy if she and her sister did end up staying at this site longer than expected. Of course, she would have to dispose of the corpses first, of which there were two. She hurried on out the door and found herself in a very long and very wide corridor. The size of this place was staggering.

Ever practical, Esperance couldn't help wondering what had happened to all the earth that had been dug out. Millions of tonnes of it! Where had they put it all?

The walls were white, the ceiling was white, the floors were white, the doors were white. Esperance assumed all this white was to compensate for the lack of sunlight down here. What it also did was make the streaks and splashes of blood stand out all the more violently.

There was a dead woman slouched up against a door. She was white with long fiery red hair. Esperance estimated that standing up she might well have been a six-footer, just like the blue test subjects. Also, she was not clad in either a lab coat or overalls. Instead, she wore blue jeans, a purple cardigan over a black t-shirt and copious amounts of jewellery. But, most intriguingly of all, this woman appeared to have not died in a frenzy of violence. Instead, she looked at peace, as if she had simply fallen asleep here.

Strange, Esperance thought. *What happened to you?*

In addition, there was something different about the door this particular body was lying against. For a start, this one had no window in it. Instead, it was emblazoned with large red letters that screamed out: 'PRIORITY 1 ONLY'.

This could mean but one thing, Esperance decided. That *it* was in there. The alien. Its face, screaming silently at her through the grille in the narrow shaft, flashed across her mind. She pushed the image away and turned to leave. But...

But...

She felt a pull. Was it a part of herself that was urging her hand to the SmartCard that hung around her neck, or was it the thing behind the door? She tried to fight this urge, but could not. She tapped her SmartCard against the little black box on the wall next to the door, but nothing happened. She tried it again. Same result. She breathed out, relieved. But still she felt the pull.

Just go, her inner voice pleaded. *Just turn around, walk away and go. Go back to Godriva, go back to Buki and get the hell off this damned island. Don't go in that room. Don't look into its eyes. Forget it exists. Just go.*

But this voice, strong though it was, could not compete against the pull that Esperance was feeling, and so she looked back to the dead woman. There was a

SmartCard hanging around her limp neck, but not like the one that Esperance had 'borrowed'. This particular SmartCard, in bright red letters, read: 'PRIORITY 1'.

Esperance crouched down next to her and examined the name badge on her cardigan. There was the SpaceWurd logo, and beneath it the words, '*Dr Kristall Jones – Liaison Officer*'.

Reverentially, Esperance removed the SmartCard from the late Ms Jones' neck, causing her head to flop to the side. She then tapped it against the little black box and the door slid open. The body of Dr Kristall Jones fell backwards and her head hit the floor with a sickening crack. Esperance winced. She was breathing in short, sharp gasps. Behind the tight wall of her chest, her heart pounded like an industrial hammer.

The door was opening and closing on the body of the dead woman now. Esperance found the sight of this as disturbing as the prospect of what awaited her beyond it. She knew she could not in good conscience leave this poor woman as she was, so she took hold of the feet, waited for the door to open and then pulled the body through to the corridor. Kristall was now lying with her arms stretched out above her head like an arrow. Out of respect to her, Esperance folded them across her chest. Then she returned to the door, which was now shut again.

Don't do this, the little voice begged. *There'll be no going back if you do this!*

But Esperance could not be persuaded. She steeled

herself, zapped it open and stepped inside. Behind her, the door slid shut. Esperance forced herself to look up and into the eyes of the alien creature standing erect behind the wall of transparent fibreglass. It pressed one of its spidery hands against the barrier that separated them and blinked.

Half a world away, Mr B, his entourage and a control room full of employees were watching in silence.

I think, whispered Esperance's inner voice, *this is what's known as a reality check moment*.

It certainly was. Exactly one week ago, Esperance had been at home with her family and everything had been (relatively) normal, and now she was about to instigate a conversation with an alien. She was standing as far away from it as she possibly could, with her back pressed up against the wall. The being blinked again. Esperance considered saying something, but 'hello' seemed catastrophically inadequate. Then the right words came...

"You said you can help us."

And with this, the mysterious creature stepped back from the clear wall and turned its head to the side. Esperance followed its gaze and her eyes fell on a little black box beyond the creature's reach, the key to its freedom.

"Before I free you," Esperance began, "I want your word that you will take myself, my sister and her baby away from this place, as you said you would."

The alien continued to stare at her for a moment, and

then it nodded.

"And you won't harm us?"

The alien shook its head. Then Esperance approached the cell wall and met the alien's gaze as an equal. She held up her Priority 1 SmartCard for it to see.

"I have the means to free you, and you in turn have the means to free us. Do we have an understanding?"

Again, the alien nodded. The enormity of the moment came crashing down on Esperance like a tidal wave. She was aware that in releasing this being she could potentially be altering the course of human history.

***

The road had been built for the sole purpose of connecting the city of Scottsdale to the spaceport. Or was it the other way around? Either way, it was eerily quiet, and Alison's car, a silver Buick Cascada convertible, was the only vehicle on it. The sun had by now set and darkness was encroaching, so she drove with the lid on.

Cynthia had given Alison a rambling and disjointed rundown of everything Neal Terry had told her. The expression on Alison's face suggested to Cynthia that she had been struggling to believe it, not that Cynthia could blame her.

But Alison had a way with words. She had the ability to cut through metres of bullshit with just a few of them, and she had done so just a few moments ago, much to Cynthia's amusement.

"You know what Byron Wurd is?" she had asked. "He's just a sad little man with a hard-on for a big machine."

Cynthia had erupted into wicked, gleeful laughter at that one. Yeah, Al was right. That's *exactly* what he was. The laughter came as a welcome distraction from the urgency of the situation they were now in, but it didn't last long and Cynthia was getting edgy again.

"Can't you go any faster?" she asked.

Alison noted her girlfriend's agitation. However, laws were laws. "The limit's fifty-five."

"But isn't this, like, a private road, or something?"

"I don't know. Is it?"

"Well, Mr B built it just for the spaceport, so I would say so."

Alison considered the logic of this. She also wondered if any cops would bother staking out a road that hardly anyone ever drove on. She decided probably not, so she put her foot down and the Buick surged forward.

"Wow! Great acceleration on this. It's like being strapped into an X-Wing Fighter!"

"No more *Star Trek* references. Please."

"Oh, Jesus."

"I'm sorry?"

"Nothing."

Cynthia's attention returned to the road ahead, and

what awaited her at the end of it. She was hoping her top tier SmartCard would get her past the guards on the gate. After that, she'd have the freedom of the spaceport. Also, she hoped she was in time.

**

"She's not going to do it, is she?" said the personal assistant.

Byron, who had not removed his Stetson despite being indoors and, indeed, deep underground, waved a dismissive hand at his underling. "She will. There's a lot riding on this, so he'll make her one way or another."

Everyone's eyes remained fixed on the giant screen before them, but their ears were now firmly tuned into whatever their boss had to say.

"And then what? What if he restarts The Machine?"

"That's what I'm hoping for."

James Sanders, Byron's PA, was a closet Democrat, a closet atheist and a closet homosexual. Any one of these would have been enough to get him fired, but he had so far managed to keep it all under the radar and retain this job which had taken him all over the world. Now he was wishing he hadn't bothered.

"Um. Mr Wurd. Is this really such a good idea?" he nervously asked. "If we're right about what happened the last time, then it could mean that…"

"A deal's a deal, Sanders," said Byron, dismissing him.

Duly dismissed, Sanders snuck off to a stairwell to make a private call. "David," he whispered, "listen very carefully to what I'm about to say and don't ask questions. Just do it. And don't tell anyone else, either. Got that? Good. Get the dogs and go to your parents' place, now. I mean right now. Don't pause, don't pack, just get in the car and get out of the city because something big is going to happen. And by big I also mean bad. Very bad."

***

Esperance tapped her SmartCard against the little black box. There was a beep, then the sound of a mechanism grinding into life. A moment later, the transparent fibreglass wall parted. Esperance took a few paces back as the alien stepped out of the cell and into freedom.

"So what now?" she asked.

The alien did not answer. Instead, it walked right past Esperance and exited the room.

"Wait! What happens now?" Esperance asked as she followed behind. "Are you going to take us to South Africa?"

Victor, it seemed, did not need a SmartCard. He could open the doors by presenting the back of his tiny wrist to the little black boxes on the walls next to them. Esperance realised then that he must have an implant. She followed him down the long corridor, past the eviscerated corpses and scattered body parts, but Victor seemed to be completely unaware of her existence.

"Wait! We had a deal! You said you'd help us!"

And still Victor walked on, down the dazzlingly bright corridor with the vivid red streaks of blood on the wall.

"Where are you going? Stop!"

He was heading for the big metallic doors at the end of the corridor, the ones marked 'NO ADMITTANCE'. He zapped his wrist against the little black box, the doors slid open and Esperance's feet were almost pulled from under her as the air was sucked out of the corridor.

"What the…?"

Then the air pressure normalised, and Victor was gone. The doors had slid shut behind him, locking Esperance out. She tapped her SmartCard against the little black box but nothing happened. She did it again. Nothing. Whatever was beyond the doors was evidently out of reach even for Priority 1 personnel.

It's the dome, the frantic voice inside Esperance's head surmised. *Whatever's in there is underneath the giant dome.*

Victor had played her and her sister for fools. The instant his cell door had opened, Esperance had ceased to matter to him. The alien was just another being who had used her as a pawn. Frustration and anger boiled up inside her like magma.

"NO!" she yelled as she kicked at the door. "NO!"

***

252

"Someone. Someone," said Byron impatiently. He clicked his fingers several times, as if issuing orders to a dog.

Mostin issued an electronic command, the big screen flickered and the image changed. There was Victor, standing on a walkway suspended over The Machine. The alien creature was tiny in comparison to this vast structure. It was a hole, perfectly round, lined with copper, riddled with electrodes and measuring roughly a hundred metres in diameter. It plunged kilometres deep into the earth, and into complete blackness.

The alien seemed to be contemplating this great abyss. He was leaning against the rail of the walkway, looking over. Then he marched on.

"He's going for the control panel," said Byron. "He's going to do it."

"Sir. Shouldn't we…?" Sanders began, but Bryon cut him off.

"One more word out of you, Sanders, and you're history."

Aren't we anyway? the PA thought.

Chapter 17

The Machine had taken years to build. For at least half a decade, Chinook helicopters, sometimes as many as twenty a day, had flown in parts and taken away earth. It had been a mammoth undertaking and a logistical nightmare.

Hundreds of labourers had been employed, each of them following very specific instructions, none of them knowing exactly what it was they were working on. They had lived some miles from the lab facility, in a compound of their own, unfenced. This had now fallen into a state of decay, the buildings having been reclaimed by nature and subsequently ravaged by the great storm of a few days previously.

And when the labourers had left, the scientists had moved in, along with the test subjects. After they had settled, the one who was ultimately overseeing the project arrived. This had caused quite a stir, somewhat understandably.

He had no name, so someone, as a mildly amusing joke, had suggested Victor. Victor had been the codename of the man who claimed to have obtained footage of an alien interview conducted at the clandestine US military base known as Groom Lake.

That footage was, of course, fake.

Victor came accompanied by a companion, a human woman named Dr Kristall Jones. Kristall was a psychic, and Victor, having no voice of his own, spoke through her. She, like the others, was dead now. But she had not been ripped apart by the rampaging test subjects. She had been killed by Victor.

When he had started The Machine that first time, Kristall had realised what Victor was up to and had tried to stop him. She had lunged for the control panel and shut it down, but not in time to stop the power surge that had fried the astronauts' minds. Then she had tried to warn the scientists and engineers about Victor's plan, so he, for want of a better phrase, had switched her off. He had accessed her mind and shut it down, but not before she had managed to lock him in the cell.

And now Victor was back at the controls, playing god with the destiny of an entire planet.

The chamber housing The Machine was vast beyond awe. The Machine itself was wider and deeper than should have been physically possible. The blackness at its core was complete. It was dormant now, but Victor was about to bring it to life so that it may achieve its purpose.

He presented the back of his wrist to the scanner on the control panel and waited as circuits thrummed into life. In order to restart The Machine, Victor would have to recalibrate it. This would take a few moments, but that was okay. The only person who could possibly have prevented him doing this was now safely locked out in the corridor.

Chapter 18

The video feed from the chamber housing The Machine to the control room in the top tier was still silent. The techies had not managed to bring the sound back online after the power outage.

The atmosphere in the control room was brittle. Over twenty pairs of eyes watched as Victor finished recalibrating The Machine. Then he activated it. He returned to the middle of the walkway and again looked down over the side, contemplating the immense black tunnel. It did not, however, stay black for long. Vertical track-lighting flickered into life, electrodes began to pulsate and, from somewhere deep in the pit, an eerie green glow emanated.

Uneasy looks were exchanged among the workers as an eager smile spread across Bryon Wurd's face. He removed his Stetson and stroked his chin in anticipation. It had begun, and this time there was nothing that could stop it.

***

"Lights ahead. Looks like this is it."

"What do you want me to do?"

"Just slow down and drive up to the gate like everything's normal. Leave the rest to me."

Alison eased off the gas. As the car slid up to the gate, a bulky man in his fifties, soft-faced and bored-looking, emerged from the cabin. She noticed he was wearing a sidearm.

"Are you sure you know what you're doing?"

"Shush."

As Cynthia always came and went by plane, she never got to know the gate guards and they never got to know her. Familiarity, always such a reliable tool, could not be relied upon here.

The guard approached and Cynthia lowered her window and smiled. "Hey," she said.

The guard lowered his head to peer into the car. He was very obviously not smiling. "Can I help you ladies?"

Cynthia played her trump card, otherwise known as her Central Security SmartCard. "I left my laptop here earlier. Just come to pick it up then we're on our way."

The guard took the SmartCard from her and held it up to the light from the spots behind him. He regarded it through narrowed eyes. Cynthia and Alison held their breaths and exchanged a look.

"Alright," said the guard as he passed the card back to its owner. "Go on through."

He slinked back into his cabin and a few seconds later the barrier lifted.

"Piece of cake," Cynthia said with a wink.

***

In the dusty grounds of the facility, the earth began to shake. Godriva was distraught. What was happening? Was it yet another earthquake or was it something worse? Where was her sister? What if this quake caused the underground labs to collapse, trapping Esperance or even killing her? What then? How could Godriva, on her own, with her baby in her arms…?

And suddenly, there was Esperance, exploding from the hatch in the ground like a shell from a bazooka. "We have to get out of here! Now!"

Godriva was having none of that. "But the blue men! They're still outside!"

They looked over at the giant steel fence. Beyond it, the few blue savages who had been loitering were running away in terror.

"They're heading for the jungle!" Esperance cried. "Now's our chance!"

Godriva grabbed her by the arm. "What happened down there? What's going on?"

"The alien tricked us! He's activated the machine and god knows what's going to happen! We need to go!"

And then, a voice from the heavens rang out.

"Hi! This is Cynthia! Remember me?"

259

The stars were just starting to twinkle in the sky as Cynthia marched into the spaceport terminal. She nodded nonchalantly at the security guy on the front desk and headed for the elevator.

"It's clobbering time," she whispered as she entered.

She didn't take it all the way down to the top tier, just as far as her old stomping ground, the monitoring station. Cynthia would have defined the mood in there at that particular moment as Mild Panic. There was an earthquake in progress at the East Africa facility. Or should that be, *another* earthquake? This one was far more severe than the previous tremors, severe enough to warrant frantic phone calls and requests for instructions should the site be compromised, etcetera, etcetera. This was good because it meant that she could slip past her former colleagues pretty much unnoticed.

However, one former colleague did notice her arrival; her old friend Matt. Just as he was about to bellow forth an enthusiastic 'HELLOOO!', Cynthia put a finger to her lips and issued a silent 'Sssh." Matt took the hint and drew a metaphorical zip across his mouth.

Cynthia clocked that Clive's office was empty (he was obviously at home, gazing lovingly at his Star Wars action figures) so she logged herself into his computer and got to work, first accessing the CCTV and loudspeaker system at the east Africa lab site.

Straightaway she could see the two women and the baby in the middle of the great big H in the middle of the compound. They looked like they were arguing, but the picture was very wobbly so it was hard to tell.

"Hi! This is Cynthia! Remember me? Listen to me very carefully, okay? I think I know a way you can get off the island, but you're gonna need a Priority 1 SmartCard! Do you think you can find one?"

The pixelated figure of Esperance held up the SmartCard that was hanging around her neck and made a display of pointing at it, telling Cynthia everything she needed to know.

"Fucking A!" she hollered, before remembering there was a baby present. "Oops. Sorry. Anyway, that's great! Now, have you found the comms room?"

Two thumbs up from Esperance.

"Good! Everything should be back online now! Find a workstation or a computer in the comms room – anyone will do – stick the SmartCard into the side of it and that should bring it online! Okay?"

Two thumbs up.

"And then here's what you do…"

***

"Why the hell does she keep sticking her thumbs up like that?"

Byron had stepped forward and was squinting at the screen. "And why's she staring into the camera? It's not as if anyone here's talking to her."

"Um, Mr Wurd," said Mostin. "According to this, the loudspeaker system has been engaged."

"Engaged? By whom?"

Mostin went back to his monitor. "Erm…Cynthia Dowley."

"So where is she? Is she here?"

"Not at the moment," said Elise. "She's on the late shift tonight so she should be on her way."

"Actually," interrupted Mostin, "she's here already. She's accessing the loudspeaker from…hang on…hang on…upstairs. Clive Rogers' desktop."

Byron's face turned beetroot. "Call security! Now!"

***

Cynthia exited the monitoring station on tiptoe, but not before having a quick and quiet word in Matt's ear.

***

Esperance raced into the comms block and crash landed in the seat at the nearest workstation. Godriva came trailing in behind her, carrying Buki in her good arm. Esperance slipped the SmartCard from her neck, reminded herself of the name on it – Dr Kristall Jones – and inserted it into the slot at the side, just as this Cynthia girl had instructed. The screen flashed into life.

A grey box came up asking for a password, but that

was okay because Cynthia had given her a hot tip. In the bottom right corner of the screen was a tiny email symbol. Esperance clicked on it. Another grey box appeared with the letters ICE above it, which stood for In Case of Emergency.

Inside the grey box was a cursor, blinking and waiting. Esperance started typing.

***

Two security personnel, one female, one male, dashed through the monitoring station in the direction of Clive's office, attracting stares from the still-mildly-panicking workers. They both had their hands on the nightsticks holstered at their sides, just in case.

The female security human-weapon was called Leigh Gryder. The name Leigh has a few meanings, 'meadow' being one and 'delicate' being another. However, there was nothing delicate about this particular Leigh. She was a mixed martial arts champ who prided herself on having never lost a fight with a man, and tonight she was busting to dish out a hiding, and she didn't much care who to.

She reached the office first, only to find it empty. "Fuck!" she rasped. "Call the front desk," she snapped.

Knowing what was good for him, her colleague Simon did as he was told.

***

As the guard on the front desk was explaining to Simon that yeah, some girl did go trotting past a few minutes ago, Cynthia and Alison were in the main hangar snapping selfies with the two Astreus spaceships.

***

"It's Colin on the front desk tonight," Simon mumbled. "He says some girl ran past…"

Leigh marched up to her colleague until she was nose to nose with him. Simon gulped.

"I *know* who's on the front desk tonight because I make it my business to know *every* night. So if the girl's already left the terminal, that means she's on her way out. And if she's on her way out, who can we call to stop her?"

Simon thought for a moment. "Erm…whoever's on the gate?"

"*Frank* is on the gate tonight, dumbass. Frank. Call him."

Simon lifted his walkie-talkie. "Frank? Oh, hey Frank. Simon. Yeah, good thanks. How are you?"

Leigh's eyes widened in a very threatening manner.

Simon collected himself. "Say, Frank. Has a girl…what? Oh, okay."

"What did he say?"

"He said to hang on a mo cos he's got to go raise the gate for someone."

And then Leigh exploded. "JESUS! FUCKING! CHRIST!"

She grabbed Simon by his shirt, pinned him against the door of Clive's disastrously empty office and…suddenly became aware that everything had fallen silent. She and Simon turned to see the entire staff of the SpaceWurd International Monitoring Station staring at them, mouths open.

"What?" said Leigh. It was more of a challenge than a question.

***

As Cynthia and Alison were zooming away from the spaceport, a silver plane swished over them, heading in the opposite direction.

"Hey! I'm supposed to be on that plane," a beaming Cynthia said.

"Does that mean you're in trouble?" asked Alison.

"Oh, I'm neck deep in it. Probably out of a job now. But I don't care, as long as those two refugees and that baby manage to get off that island. God, I hope this works."

Alison put a hand on her girlfriend's knee and gave it a squeeze. "I'm very proud of you," she said.

"Does that mean I'm forgiven for filling your fruit bowl with M&Ms?"

"You are. You know, when you were telling Heather and I about the East Africa laboratory and the refugees, it all seemed so abstract, so far away. But these are real people with real lives, and they're in danger, and you helped them."

"Yeah. I did, didn't I?"

"You are officially my hero of the day."

"That's a Metallica song," Cynthia smiled.

"I know. You've made me listen to it God knows how many times."

"It's a classic though, ain't it?"

"Well, it's no 'I Wanna Dance With Somebody', but it isn't bad."

"Wanna pull over and make out?"

Alison was shocked by such a suggestion. "No I do not want to pull over and make out! All I can think of right now is getting home and having a cup of tea."

"Don't suppose I can come and join you, can I? No job means no apartment. Gonna have to start looking around for a new situation."

"You don't sound too worried about it."

"Nah. Something'll turn up."

The opening bass riff of Megadeth's Peace Sells forced its way from the pocket of Cynthia's jeans. "Told ya," she said.

She pulled out her cell and checked the screen. "Oh, fuck. It's work."

***

The image was doing more than just wobbling now, it

266

was shaking violently, and the green glow from the hellish pit was intensifying. But despite the breaking down of the picture quality the assembled audience, among them a certain Texan billionaire called Byron Wurd, could still make out the alien known as Victor. He was still in the centre of the walkway, gazing down into the abyss that was now throbbing with emerald light, quite possibly admiring his handiwork.

"What's he up to?" Byron muttered. "Why ain't he getting the hell outta there?"

"Perhaps nothing's going to happen," Sanders nervously ventured. "Perhaps it's just another test."

Byron shot him a withering glance, delivered from the corner of his eye. "Yeah. You keep telling yerself that," he sneered.

"She's not picking up. Damn her!" seethed Elise, lowering her phone.

"Keep tryin'," Byron commanded.

"Mr B!" yelped Mostin, before correcting himself. "Erm…I mean, Mr Wurd! Look!"

Forks of lightening were now streaking out from the emerald glow, whipping into the air, striking the walls and the walkway and sending sparks flying. And still the alien stood watching.

"He just ain't movin'," Byron observed.

Elise's cell rang. "Yes?" She let out an exasperated sigh. "Right."

"What is it?"

"Cynthia exited the main gate a few minutes ago."

"Can't anyone do anything right 'round here?" Byron complained. "Where are the refugee women now?"

Mostin brought up the CCTV feed from the facility grounds in an inset on the big screen. The two women were exiting the comms room and heading for the middle of the giant H. Then one of them, the one without the baby, lowered herself in through the hatch.

"She's heading for the airlock," Mostin confirmed.

"They'll never get past the emergency door," Elise said with a smirk. "The monitors upstairs are under strict instructions not to let anyone in or out."

***

Esperance opened the hatch in the middle of the helicopter landing area. "Come! Quickly!" she ordered.

"I'll just go and get…" Godriva began.

"No! No time to get anything." Esperance barked. "We're leaving."

Yes, they were. The tremor in the earth had grown to a shudder which itself had grown to a full-blown quake. Something big was going to happen, they could feel it. Buki started screaming. Evidently, he could feel it too.

Esperance climbed down first. "Pass him down!" she ordered.

Godriva, her right arm still causing her pain, passed her crying baby down to her sister, then she clambered down behind. They reached the bottom of the ladder to find that the massive steel door was closed. The sisters weren't too worried though. Cynthia had warned them that it would be.

***

Down in the top tier, the CCTV POV on the big screen switched to the airlock. One of the refugee women was already in there, baby in arms, and the other one was clambering down the ladder.

"See?" said Elise with an icy smile. "Closed." And then the door started to swing open. Elise's jaw dropped almost to the ground. "What the…?"

Byron was not amused. "Who's opening the FUCKING DOOR?" he roared.

***

Matt leaned back in his chair with his hands behind his head and a big, satisfied smile on his face.

***

Elise was shocked. Mostin was shocked. Everyone was shocked. Up until this very moment, no one had ever heard Byron Wurd swear.

"It must be the Cynthia girl," Elise replied with a certain amount of fear in her voice.

Through his heavily lined eyes, Bryon shot her a

look. "She's already left, genius."

"You! Close it! Now!" Elise commanded.

Mostin's hand poised over his mouse, but something inside stopped him.

"You heard the lady," Bryon rumbled. "Close the damn door!"

There were only two reasons why Byron Wurd should want these two young women and the baby dead. One: he didn't want them getting off the island and blabbing about everything they'd seen. And two: he wanted to spite the girl who had let them into the site in the first place, the one who had been causing him all these problems tonight. Neither of these reasons were good enough for Mostin. He knew that if he crossed that line and closed the steel door he would cease to be mere employee and would instead become an accessory to murder. Right now, he was asking himself some very hard questions.

"I said shut it!" Byron snapped. He was not used to having to wait for his orders to be acted on.

If Mostin did 'shut it', how would he ever be able to look his wife and children in their beautiful eyes again? After all, these two women were someone's daughters too. And the baby! Oh god, the baby! How could he?

He imagined himself delivering a feeble defence of his actions in a tribunal or a court: "I was just following orders."

Yeah. That old chestnut. I was just following orders, like the Nazi concentration camp guards used to say.

Well, not anymore.

"Godammit!" Byron growled. "Get outta my way!"

Byron moved for the mouse on Mostin's desk, but Mostin stood up, putting himself in the way of his billionaire boss. Elise drew breath. Every member of Byron's entourage drew breath. Every man and woman sat at a workstation drew breath.

Over Mostin's shoulder Byron saw, on the flickering screen, the two women and the baby slip through the doorway and into the tunnel to freedom. He returned his gaze to the insubordinate standing before him.

"You're fired," he rumbled.

Mostin sighed. *Ah well,* he thought. *It was fun while it lasted.* He retrieved his jacket from the back of his chair and strolled casually towards the elevator. Then another desk-jockey got up and made for the elevator. Then another. And another. Mostin's act of defiance had inspired a mass walkout.

"Um. Sir?" It was Sanders, and he sounded terrified.

"What is it?" Byron seethed.

Sanders was staring at his tablet computer, its glow illuminating his face which had turned a morbid shade of grey.

"Erm...you've had an email come though, sir. It's from Clive Rogers' desktop but signed off by this Cynthia Dowley girl."

Byron turned to his PA and fixed him with a threatening stare. "Well? What does it say?"

"It says: 'Dear Bryon. You're just a sad little man

271

with a hard-on for a big machine. Love, Cynthia'."

Byron turned back to the CCTV feed from the airlock, which was now empty. He rubbed his eyes and sighed. "Shut it," he murmured.

"But I didn't say anything," said Elise.

"I meant the door."

Elise used Mostin's computer to order the door to shut. Then she picked up her cell. "I'll try her again," she said before hitting Cynthia's number.

"One of those refugees saw the alien," said Byron, his voice heavy with resignation. "It spoke to them. If they make it back to civilisation and start talking…Jesus fucking Christ."

***

The massive steel door swung inwards, letting in the stench of death and a swarm of flies. There in the tunnel were the shredded remains of the boy beyond the fence, and feasting on them a party of large rats. Esperance and Godriva recoiled in horror.

"Oh god. Oh god. I can't," Godriva stammered as she backed away from the grisly sight. "I can't."

Esperance took her hand. "Close your eyes," she said. "This whole place could collapse in on us any moment so we can't afford to hang around."

The ground was shaking violently as she led her sister past the blood, guts, bones and rats. In her other arm she held Buki who was by now as distraught as his

272

mother.

"Nearly there," she said. "Nearly there."

***

Finally, The Machine achieved its purpose. Beyond the dome, the giant satellite dish, which wasn't in fact a satellite dish at all, swivelled on its housing and tilted its feed horn up towards the sky. The air crackled with static electricity as a laser beam, green and intense, burst upwards. It sliced through the atmosphere and began its journey into deep space at a speed incomprehensible to the human mind, carrying with it the molecules belonging to the alien known as Victor.

The white noise of static ricocheted across the plain, bringing Esperance and Godriva skidding to a halt. They turned to see the green laser beam slicing through the bright blue sky.

"What is it?" gasped an incredulous Godriva.

"The Machine," Esperance replied. "Heaven help us."

Then something cataclysmic happened. With a thunderous BOOM the roof of the dome shattered outwards, sending shards of burning metal high into the sky.

"RUN!" Esperance yelled. They turned on their heels and sprinted away from the site that had been their home for the last four days. Seconds later, a chunk of dome the size of a bus impacted into the ground where they had just been standing. This was followed by more pieces of dome, some of them aflame. They were plummeting to the ground all around the fleeing sisters now.

"Make for the outcropping!" Esperance yelled.

Godriva felt a twinge in her shoulder. "No!" she yelled back. "Go around it and head for the jungle!"

"But that's where the blue men are!"

"And the boat!"

Esperance had forgotten all about the lifeboat, which was – hopefully – still where they had left it. They adjusted their course accordingly and sprinted like cheetahs into the fresh morning.

Meanwhile, far above their heads, the window that had allowed them to see into the furthest reaches of cold, dead space was opening.

***

The enormous screen was now blank. The CCTV camera housed in the huge, arcing dome had been vaporised, along with Victor. A stunned silence had fallen upon the control room. Most of the employees had walked out, leaving only a few hangers-on, as well as Elise, Byron and his entourage.

"He just stood there and let himself die," Sanders muttered.

"No," Byron said. "It's just his body that died. His mind is still out there somewhere."

"What? Are you serious?"

"I am."

The government attaché stepped forward. "Alien bodies are just vessels. It was no more a part of Victor than a diving suit would be a part of you."

"Jesus," was all Sanders could say.

The attaché's phone, which had not left his hand this whole time, buzzed. He looked at the screen. As usual, his poker face gave nothing away.

"Yes?"

Then he handed the phone to Bryon. "It's the Pentagon," he said. "They want an update."

Chapter 19

"Pull over here," said Cynthia.

"But we're in the middle of nowhere."

"I know, and it's beautiful."

Alison did so and they exited the car. It was cold so Cynthia zipped up her leather jacket and Alison her Canada Goose Shelburne Parka.

"You're right," Alison said. "It is beautiful."

The sky was a deep, luxurious shade of purple, streaked with wisps of red cloud, reflecting the last remaining rays of the sun. Above them, stars twinkled vividly as there was no light out here in the desert to pollute the sky. They were alone, save for the tumbleweeds, cacti and distant columns of rock. Alison leant against the grille of her car. As it warmed up her behind, Cynthia cuddled up against her.

"Don't suppose there's any jobs going with you at the research centre," she ventured.

Alison hooked an arm through Cynthia's. "Don't worry about it. I make enough money for both of us."

Cynthia's eyes brightened. "Alison Lloyd. Is that

your way of asking if I wanna move in with you?"

"Could be," replied Alison with a warm smile. "Of course, you're going to have to cut down on the hot dogs and video games."

"Yeah. And you're gonna have to lower your standards. And what about my boyfriend?"

"Mashed Potato can come too."

"Damn right he can. We come as a package deal."

A shooting star raced across the cold, clear sky.

"Make a wish," Alison said.

"I did, and it just came true."

And then something else streaked across the sky, something far more dramatic than a shooting star.

"Oh. My. Fucking. God."

***

The jungle was ahead of them now, and beyond that the beach, the place where this nightmare had begun. The sky became suddenly dark. Esperance looked up and stopped dead. Godriva followed the line of her sister's gaze and screeched to a halt.

"It can't be!" she gasped.

But it was; a spaceship, huge, grey and ring-shaped, just as they'd seen a few nights previously. It was here, just beyond the reach of Earth's gravitational pull, and it was dominating the sky. Then, the sky was sliced in two by a green laser beam and a second ring-shaped craft appeared from nowhere, riding it. The laser faded out, leaving the vessel floating in the void. This one appeared closer.

Even the baby was silent, infected by the fear and awe emanating like radiation from his mother and aunt. From somewhere came the sound of shrieking. Esperance and Godriva looked back to see four giant blue savages sprinting their way from the direction of the plain.

"GO!" Esperance cried.

***

Damning protocol, every single spaceport worker had left his or her post and had come outside, mingling with the night monitors who had not long exited the silver plane. The runway was crowded with people, all of them looking to the heavens.

The night sky was dominated by two ring-shaped spaceships; immense, threatening and alien. Matt pulled the phone from his pocket and called home. So did a few others. Most of the observers, however, had their phones trained on the incredible event occurring above them and were live-streaming it to the world. If there was any talk at all, it was hushed and reverential.

The brittle stillness was violently shattered by a screeching so loud it hurt. People ducked, fearing an attack. But the terrible noise did not have an alien origin. Two F-16 fighter jets streaked overhead, and as they did so another laser sliced through the sky and a third spaceship appeared. It rode along its laser for a few moments before halting. Then the laser faded away.

Sanders looked to his boss, Byron Wurd, the man who had dominated his life for the last ten years. "What the fuck have you done?" he asked.

***

Lasers were appearing at regular intervals now, each one heralding the coming of yet another ring-shaped craft, and with each arrival the sky grew ever darker. The light of day had all but gone by the time Esperance and Godriva, both running for their lives, hit tree cover.

"BUKI!" screamed Godriva.

"I have him!" Esperance shouted back. "Stay close to me!"

A ferocious wind whipped through the jungle, almost knocking the sisters of their feet.

"WHAT IS THAT?" Godriva screamed. "WHAT'S HAPPENING?"

"JUST STAY CLOSE TO ME!"

Esperance's call was accompanied by Buki's screaming.

"ESPERANCE! BUKI!"

"WE'RE HERE!"

The jungle interior was a tangle of roots, vines, confusion, darkness and chaos. Branches were flying and trees falling as the noise rocketed to an agony-inducing decibel. Fearing she was about to be blown away, Godriva wrapped her arms around the thick trunk of a tree, closed her eyes and prayed.

There was a crackle of electricity followed by a brief scream. But the scream had not come from either Buki or Esperance. Godriva squinted into the furious murkiness. Three blue men rushed by like a pack of panicking dogs. What had happened to the fourth?

The hairs on the back of Godriva's neck prickled as a flash of electricity ripped through the trees, reducing one of the terrified savages to atoms. As he ceased to exist, he just about had time to issue a shriek.

And then there were two.

For a blissful moment, Godriva wondered if help had finally arrived, but then her feet lifted up from the floor and a new wave of panic kicked in. Her body became fully horizontal and she was clinging to the tree not just for sanctuary but for her life. She was in the grip of an incredible force. It was pulling her. It wanted her.

The noise of the wind rose until it became a howl that scratched and clawed at the inside of Godriva's head. Through the blizzard of branches and roots and vines she saw three lights. They were round and full, and in each of them was a silhouette. The silhouettes were humanoid in shape, with spindly limbs and large, bulbous heads.

They were here. They were real.

This was a nightmare against which her mind had no defence, and Godriva screamed as she had never screamed before. She refused to accept that such things could be in the world, in *her* world. It was an abomination in Godriva's eyes. How dare they? How dare they exist! Her terror gave way to madness as her grip slipped and her nightmare reached its crescendo. Her body was in horizontal freefall, hurtling towards the light and the waiting aliens. Her last thought was of her son, Buki.

None of this would be remembered by him, of course. He wouldn't start retaining explicit memories until his second year, which was still a year-and-a-half away. He would have no recollection of the blue savages, of the facility, or – god willing – of Victor. Nor would he have any recollection of the stealth helicopters or of the soldier clad entirely in black who aimed a gun at his aunt's head.

Esperance cleared the trees and emerged onto the beach, relieved. It had been madness in there; the force had been strong enough to tear trees out of the ground by their roots, but still it wasn't over. The sound of splintering wood tore through her as something big rose out of the trees. It was a large pill-shaped craft, silver. As it hovered over the jungle it slowly revolved and Esperance saw three round lights on the side. Were they lights or were they windows? Then she noticed shapes moving in the lights. She held the screaming baby close to her chest and backed away.

In her head was a single thought: *Godriva*.

The mysterious craft suddenly shot upwards into the sky. Esperance knew then that she had lost her sister forever, and Buki his mother. She turned and ran towards the sea, and that's when the Lockheed Raider X helicopters swooped in.

There were two of them, black, like nothing Esperance had ever seen before. They descended and landed in seconds, spilling out their cargo of black-clad Special Forces soldiers. One of them raised his M4A1 in the direction of Esperance's head and fired. Esperance felt a stream of bullets brush past her ear. In her shock, she turned to see a blue savage that she didn't even know was behind her collapse into the sand. He had no face left to speak of, or with. Esperance was too stunned even to scream.

The soldier grabbed Esperance by the arm and pulled her towards the chopper.

"Come with me!" he shouted above the shriek of the fighter jets that were now tearing up the sky overhead. "We're getting you out of here!"

Esperance was not in control anymore. She felt like a pinball ricocheting around inside a machine, bouncing off obstacles, tumbling into holes. All she could do was cling onto Buki.

Don't let him go, no matter what.

She was pushed into a seat and a belt was drawn around her waist, and then the beach was disappearing beneath her. She was over the sea now, and it was whizzing by in a blur. There was a soldier to her side and one in front. He was the one who had shot past her, killing the blue savage. Esperance could see nothing of him except his eyes, and even they were protected by goggles. But in a gesture of trust, he yanked them off and pulled down his face covering.

"Dr Kristall Jones?" he asked.

Esperance, still in a state of numb shock, nodded.

"We got your message. Your call for help. Are you injured?"

She shook her head.

"And the baby?"

She shook her head again.

"Are there any other survivors?"

A tear rolled down her cheek. "No," she said, her bottom lip quivering. "No more survivors."

Esperance leaned out and looked back at the beach, which was fast receding into the distance. She could see the second chopper and the tiny black dots of the remaining soldiers disappearing into the trees, but it was too late. Godriva was gone.

"Intel didn't say anything about a baby," the soldier said.

Esperance thought quickly. "He was born on site," she shouted above the whine of the rotor blades.

"Okay. Well, you're both safe now," said the soldier as yet another green laser cut across the sky.

Chapter 20

Back in Scottsdale, the streets were filled with shouting and screaming, panic and confusion. Somewhere, a car shuddered to a halt in the middle of the road. The car behind it crashed into the back of it. The one behind that also crashed. But there were no arguments amongst the drivers: No flailing arms and accusations or threats. They just emerged slowly from their vehicles and stared up at the sky.

Gene the hot dog wizard had his family around him; his wife Juana, his son Antonio, his daughter-in-law Adriana, and his granddaughter Rosa.

"Gonna have to rewrite the dictionary when all this is over," Gene said.

"What do you mean?" Juana asked.

"Cos I've just discovered a whole new definition o' shitting my pants."

Even in the midst of a major turning point in the history of the world, Gene's sense of humour remained intact. Valuing this quality more than ever at this particular moment, Juana snuggled into him as she contemplated the alien spaceships above them.

"I wonder if they like hot dogs?" she ventured.

Ed, now unemployed and effectively homeless since his wife had kicked him out of the family home, staggered out of his Old Town motel room and into the cold night. He, like pretty much everyone else on the planet, looked up at the sky and wondered if there would still be a planet left for him to live on when the sun came up the next day. At the very least, an alien invasion would make his own problems seem a hell of a lot smaller, and for this breadcrumb of mercy he was grateful. Then he heard the door click behind him and realised he had locked himself out in his underpants.

Heather, Cynthia and Alison's dreadlocked guitarist friend, did not stir from her deep slumber, even as a fleet of alien spacecraft assembled in orbit around the Earth. The world was changing forever, but right now she was tearing it up on stage in the arena of her dreams.

Chapter 21

In the belly of the twin-hulled FSF-1 Sea Fighter positioned somewhere between Madagascar and her own personal island of nightmares, Esperance was enduring a cursory physical examination from a coldly forensic navy medic.

This navy medic, with blonde hair scraped back into a severe ponytail, mumbled the results from the ECG machine as she noted them down. Despite Esperance's pleas, she did not share them.

"Please. I'm a nurse too," Esperance said, but she might as well have been speaking to a rock.

And then a man in khakis walked in. He was about fifty years old, Esperance reckoned, and did not look happy. He glared at Esperance from under his khaki cap. She knew he must be someone important because the medic stopped what she was doing and saluted him.

"Relieved," he said flatly.

The medic left.

The soldier had in his hand a tablet computer. When he had finished glaring at Esperance he raised it, swiped the screen and gazed at it for a few seconds. Esperance gulped and picked up Buki.

"Dr Kristall Jones?" the soldier said.

"Yes," replied a trembling Esperance.

"I'm Marine Corp General David McBailey. Are you injured, ma'am?"

"No," Esperance said with a shudder.

"And the baby?"

Esperance shook her head.

The General went back to his tablet. "According to SpaceWurd's records," he began, "Dr Kristall Jones is Caucasian. With all due respect, ma'am, you are not, which leads me to suspect that you have been somewhat less than completely honest with us."

Esperance looked down.

"Given that I just sent a team in to rescue you, I think the least you owe me is a straight answer. So, who are you really?"

Buki was looking up at Esperance. She gazed into his longing eyes and could not bear the thought of this poor baby growing up without his mother, so she came to a decision. A drastic, life-changing decision.

"My name is Godriva Watara," she said. "And this is my son Bukeneza. Buki for short."

The General's poker-face remained unmoved. "And where are you from, Miss Watara?"

"Bujumbura in Burundi."

"Refugee?"

Esperance, now Godriva, nodded.

"And where were you going?"

"South Africa, to start a new life with my baby."

"How long were you in the facility?"

Esperance began to wonder if this was actually an interrogation as opposed to just someone asking questions.

"Four days," she said sadly.

The General paused. "Did you see it?" he eventually asked. "And if you did, then you won't need me to clarify what *it* is."

How Esperance chose to answer this question could have very serious repercussions, she knew. Would she be dooming herself by answering honestly? Would she be dooming herself by lying and insisting she'd seen nothing? Her mind grappled with a million possible outcomes, but she was tired – so very tired – and maintaining a lie requires energy. Unfortunately, her reserves were depleted.

"Yes," she said. "I saw it."

"Did it communicate with you in any way?"

"It spoke to us – to my sister and I – through Buki." She raised the baby a little.

"I see. And where is your sister now?"

"She didn't make it."

The General removed his cap to reveal a head of short, paper-white hair. "I'm very sorry to hear that, ma'am."

Esperance said nothing. But then, from nowhere, inspiration struck.

"I saw the planet the alien came from. It appeared one night above the facility."

The general sounded sceptical. "You saw a planet above the facility?"

"Yes. Every night a window appeared that allowed us to see where the alien came from. We saw its planet. There were lights on it. I filmed it on my phone."

The general considered this for a moment, and then said, "Well now, that makes you just about the most important person I've spoken to today, and a few hours ago I was on the phone to the president. So, how about this? In return for a comprehensive account of everything that happened in that facility over the last four days, along with any pertinent footage you may have on your phone, I will personally guarantee safe passage to South Africa for yourself and your baby. Do we have a deal?"

Esperance stared at him with disbelieving eyes. "You really mean it?"

"Yes I do, ma'am." He really did.

"Yes. We have a deal," she said. Then she started crying and didn't stop for many hours.

***

Out on the lonely desert road, Cynthia wondered if Alice Cooper was standing in the street outside his Arizona home and staring up at the heavens. Of course he was. Who in the world wasn't right now, other than

Heather? Cynthia took a small amount of comfort in this thought, that she was sharing a significant moment with a genuine rock god, despite the fact he was completely unaware of it. She sighed.

"Are you okay?" Alison asked.

"Ask me again tomorrow," Cynthia replied. "So, what do you think's gonna happen now? I mean, to all of us? To the world?"

She felt Alison's fingers entwine with her own. "I don't know. But whatever does, we'll face it together."

THE END

Acknowledgements

The author would like to thank…

My parents, for filling my head with stories and music when I was young. My family and friends, for being my family and friends. Everyone in Swansea and District Writers Circle, for their unending support and infectious enthusiasm. Everyone at The Wave and the old Swansea Sound, for the camaraderie and good times. The following people for helping me over the bumps in the road: Jan Ellis, Dr Helen Locking, Claire Pearson, Val Penny and Lady Andrea. And lastly, everyone at Cranthorpe Millner, for believing in me and in Frenzy Island.

About the author

Portrait by Tia Sandry

Richard E. Rock is a professional writer. By day he works as a commercial scriptwriter in the radio industry and by night composes dark and fantastical books. The inspiration for his hair-raising stories comes from his nightmares, which he deliberately induces. His interests include Norwegian Black Metal, Russian prison literature and Scooby Doo. He lives in South Wales with his girlfriend and their cat. Frenzy Island is his second novel.